穿孔城市
PERFORATED CITY

策展人
黃海鳴

Curator
Hai-Ming Huang

-

偕同策展人
黃香凝

Co-Curator
Anita Hsiang-Ning Huang

目錄

序文

「穿孔城市」展覽專刊序
駱麗真｜台北當代藝術館館長
008

策展論述

「穿孔城市」的再思考
黃海鳴｜策展人
014

專文

失落的地龍國：一座穿孔中的城市憂鬱
高千惠｜藝術書寫者
032

在流動的縫隙之間──
行走「穿孔城市」的策展閱讀
張晴文｜國立清華大學藝術與設計學系助理教授
046

圖錄

第一組
社會網絡關係的固著 /
脫落 / 糾結牽制

陳伯義
060

洪譽豪
066

朱駿騰
072

陳宣誠
078

姚瑞中
084

第二組
社會邊緣人藝術家
自組具有影響力的關係網絡

陳毅哲
092

鄧雯馨
098

林羿綺
104

唐唐發 + FIDATI [PINDY WINDY]
110

第三組
以不同高度、
速度運動及工作的物種

鄧堯鴻
118

黃彥超
124

許惠晴
130

第四組
難以掙脫歷史迷障的回歸？

梁廷毓
138

張徐展
144

顏忠賢
150

郭奕臣
156

吳宜樺
164

郭俞平
170

藝術家簡歷
178

Contents

Foreword

Foreword to *Perforated City*
LiChen Loh | Director of Museum of
Contemporary Art, Taipei
008

Exhibition Discourse

Re-visiting *Perforated City*
Hai–Ming Huang | Curator
014

Essays

The Lost Earthly Dragon Kingdom:
The Melancholy of a Perforated City
Chien-Hui KAO | Art Author
032

Between the Changing Crevasses:
Curatorial Readings on *Perforated City*
Chang Ching-Wen | Assistant Professor,
Department of Arts and Design,
National Tsing Hua University
046

Plates

Group 1
Fixation, Split and Entanglement of
Social Relations and Networks

Chen Po-I
060

Yu-Hao Hung
066

Chu ChunTeng
072

Eric Chen
078

YAO Jui-Chung
084

Group 2
The Influential Relationship Network
Formed by Socially Marginal Artists

Yi-Che, Chen
092

Teng Wen-Hsin
098

LIN, Yi-Chi
104

Tang Tang-Fa + FIDATI (PINDY WINDY)
110

Group 3
Varied Species Moving and
Working at Different Altitude
and Speed

Deng Yau-Horng
118

Huang Yen-Chao
124

HSU, HUI-CHING
130

Group 4
Returning to the Inescapable
Haze of History?

Liang Ting-Yu
138

ZHANG XU zhan
144

Yan Chung-Hsien
150

KUO I-Chen
156

WU Yi-Hua
164

Kuo Yu-Ping
170

Artist Biographies
178

Foreword

序文 ⓪

一剖城市之遞嬗聯結

文｜駱麗真

「穿孔城市」展覽由長期關注臺灣當代藝術發展之資深策展人黃海鳴策畫，以傳統舊式的集合式住宅建物「步登公寓」為引，剖析屬於都市人們生活的紋理，透過漫步虛實空間，爬梳屬於這座城市的過往記憶。

策展人黃海鳴假「穿孔」一詞，擴大傳統對於空間討論之框架，以被切開的乳酪作為思考意象，那隨著時間逐漸發霉或酸臭狀態，正是多元城市風貌所展現出之一座隨機取樣的橫剖面。黃海鳴像是城市中的漫遊者，透過其長期對於城市觀察所培養出的敏銳視角，垂直穿梭於存在與不存在等各異質場域，討論現代人因生理或心理空間狀態變化，而隨之引發的集體記憶與動態關係。

展覽規劃共包含四項子題：透過實體城市建築物的興建與頹圮，以及有機違章建築的增生與蔓延，一方面觀察城市風貌的轉變與再生；另一方面，則在過程當中，發掘人們根據空間分隔與私有化的改變，隨之因應流動與創造連結的生活樣態與群聚行為；而虛擬世界的發展所帶來的全球化與數位化，使得雲端生活所混合帶來的便利與隱形的災難與危機，就像是裹著糖衣的誘餌，在享受科技帶來的進步同時，也有塊未竟之地正在悄悄地產生風化、質變；處在其中的人們，面對這些看似再平凡不過的日常，又該如何整理及回望自己的本心。

本次展覽共邀請 18 組藝術家參與，他們以創作為餌，化身為城市中的引路人，帶領觀眾潛入城市的表面與內裡，以藝術的手法擷取城市的生活切面，揭露城市夾縫中關於公寓聚落、族群遷徙、人鬼異族、政治傷痕、底層移民等行為活動的記憶與想像。

本檔展覽推出期間，正值嚴重特殊傳染性肺炎 COVID-19 防疫期間，本館因應大環境變化，也首度推出「藝術宅在家線上導覽」服務，邀請策展人與藝術家進行線上導覽服務，為即將到來的新日常，開啟未來與觀眾溝通的新方法。對照本檔展覽所開啟的討論，似乎某些甚麼在此獲得證實。

一檔展覽的完整呈現，除了策展人與館內同仁、工讀生、志工等行政團隊的戮力以赴，更感謝以下贊助單位的共襄盛舉：THERMOS 膳魔師、驕陽基金會、當代藝術基金會、東和鋼鐵企業股份有限公司、春之文化基金會、老爺會館、SABON，同時感謝台灣愛普生高階專業投影機和臺灣三星電子的硬體贊助，以及萬田金屬工程、弘采介護有限公司與建成國中的特別參與，讓本檔展覽得以順利圓滿地展現在每一位觀眾眼前。

Slice a Piece of Urban Transformation and Interconnection

Text | LiChen Loh

The exhibition *Perforated City* is curated by Hai-Ming Huang, an experienced curator who has long devoted his attention to the development of the Taiwanese contemporary art scene. Unfolding the discussion with traditional multi-dwelling unit "walk-up apartments," the exhibition analyses the texture of urbanites' lives, assembling the memories of this city through wandering between virtual and physical spaces.

The curator Hai-Ming Huang expands the limitation of the traditional discourse on space by adopting the term "perforated." With a piece of sliced cheese as its imagery, the state of gradually growing mold and the scent of sourness as the time goes by, is in fact a section view of any random selected diverse city. Haung is like an urban flâneur, vertically traveling through existed or non-existed heterogeneous fields. With his sensitivity long cultivated by his observance of the city, he examines the relationships between the collective memory and actions caused by the change of the physical or mental space.

The exhibition includes four subtopics: observing the alternation and rebirth of the city through the rise and fall its constructions and the spreading of organic illegal buildings; discovering the transformation of space separation and privatization, along with the ways of living and cluster effect brought by mobility and networking; the blooming of the virtual world encourages globalization and digitalization, yet like a sugar-coated bait, behind the convenience due to the technology lies quietly the forthcoming disasters and crisis; as the abovementioned issues are only a normality of our daily lives, how can one cohabitate with it while staying true to oneself.

The exhibition invites 18 groups of artists, guiding the audience diving into façade and the core of the urban through their artwork, revealing the memory and imagination of the city about residential clusters, migration, specters, political scars, the bottom social class immigrants and more.

As the exhibition coincided with the Novel Coronavirus COVID-19 Epidemic, we launched our virtual museum tours for the very first time, inviting the curator and the artists to convey online tours. This new means of communication, as it has now become the new normal, seems to mirroring the discussions of this exhibition.

The exhibition is made possible by the effort of the curator, our staff, trainees and volunteers, and moreover, our special thanks to our Sponsors: THERMOS, Sunpride Foundation, Contemporary Art Foundation, Tung Ho Steel, Spring Foundation, Royal Inn and SABON. We thank EPSON Taiwan for sponsoring us high-performance projectors and Samsung Taiwan hardware sponsorship, as well as Wan Tian Metal Project, Theralife and Jian Cheng Junior High School's participation, so that the exhibition can be successfully brought to the audience.

Exhibition
Discourse

策 展 論 述　　⃝

「穿孔城市」的再思考

文｜黃海鳴

展覽不能停在開幕的那一天，展覽後帶有距離的整體思考是非常重要的，雖然這是一個很艱難的時刻以及很累人很難再啟動的工作！

●前言

穿孔和不可避免的硬體破舊的命運有關，但是穿孔城市策展中的核心關懷是個體或群體在穿越不同的介質時的存在經驗，這必然是一種複雜的關係與過程，包括：不同的環境、不同的時代、不同的神話、不同的階層，不同的速度、不同的阻礙。不同的個體或群體在其中主動、被動，上升、下沉，麻醉、覺醒，或一邊運行一邊演化，或一邊運行一邊崩解，或一邊受挫一邊振作。有時進行不同的擴散與連結，有時遭遇不同的游離、隔離或阻礙。簡單的說，穿孔城市或穿孔城鎮，是一個讓各種關係現形的平台以及介質。

接下來將以四個不同但又相關的面向來發展以及整理，我們個別發展，但也隨時關注相互的關係。這個展覽最初只是被美術館指定為對於空間的思考，而我們選擇的主要關注是社會稍底層的複雜時空因果關係網絡，另外，相對於當初的策展過程，已經又衍生出新的提問。

●第一組：社會網絡關係的固著／脫落／糾結牽制

1. 陳伯義：《步移景換・華江陰陽》
原本只是河邊的一整塊包括住屋、農田、菜園的傳統農村聚落，在區域及整體的城鄉發展後穿越其間的大馬路，特別是高速及高架的立體運輸系統，硬生生切割了原來關係密切的鄰里，非常具有創意的環形陸橋、騎樓所結合的華江整宅，相當程度保護了原有的人與人以及人與環境的共同體關係。藝術家經過特別的藝術手法，在老舊以及冷清的華江整宅中，召喚出原有的騎樓間不同樓層間各戶人家所共享屋外植栽、所共享內外空間交織穿透的共同體人情趣味。

2. 洪譽豪：《無以為家》
這件作品在昏暗的展場中創造了古老社區巷道騎樓中某種相互交織纏繞、一不留神就會進入鄰居私人空間的親密迷宮感覺。另外藝術家也利用展場兩個背光的門口，以及走廊上另一位藝術家陳伯義很有穿透感的騎樓影像，讓這一區域的美術館轉化成公共空間、私人空間難以區分的狀態。另外當然是藝術家的拿手戲，透過走廊騎樓空間、生活物件裝置，以及銜接在一起的動態影像，將原先緊密連結的居住空間逐漸崩解，應該連偶而回來的靈魂都會覺得荒涼及陌生。

3. 朱駿騰：《八月十五》

這件作品，從八月十五那一天一位從療養院走失後再也沒有回來的失智病人的事件開始，而其中主要動態影像的主角，是一位因為患阿茲海默症失智而不斷漫走的老婦人。藝術家提到：「準備作品的一年裡，密集接觸這些因各種原因而對記憶與認知錯位的朋友與家屬……但隨著時間，我漸漸看到自己，也開始體會這些所謂『生病的遺忘』其實只是每天都會發生在我們身上的日常。」於社區周邊或甚至社區內部，很多人其實生活在各自的平行世界。前面兩件作品似乎在說社會發展造成共同體的崩解，而《八月十五》告訴我們衰老、疾病、失智或其他許多內在因素讓許多鄰近的人隔離在不同的平行世界之中。

4. 陳宣誠：《剖視島》

和藝術家分享過「將老舊公寓剖開將會是最有意思的劇場」的想法，這當然和他用竹鷹架製作的《邊境地景》有一定的延伸。建築領域的陳宣誠並沒有鎖定在老舊的公寓，也沒有強調其中的懷舊情感，反而是投向未來社會的共居共感的思考，他說：「集合公寓的不同剖面而形成多孔洞，讓不同位置間的相互連結，成為新的可能性」。經過非常複雜細緻溝通調整，最後具有大格局標題的《剖視島》作品的開放結構，與反思科技強制性的郭奕臣、與反思普遍平行世界現象的朱駿騰的作品，巧妙的結合成一體。也和稍遠的吳宜樺、郭俞平批判性極高的作品，以及穿越地板和樓下鄧堯鴻的大老鼠乾產生有趣對話。

5. 姚瑞中：《巨神連線》

藝術家透過收集全國各地信徒們的「巨大慾力」巨大神像的投射物，共構出臺灣地理空間內緊密交織的常民生活、信仰文化、與政治經濟關係。藝術家強調作品拍攝視角，企圖傳達我們突然在行進中被超乎尋常的巨大神像震攝的狀態，三頻道大幅投影展示更要讓影像具有震攝力。我認為聲響的運用是同樣重要的：發出巨大音量的美國國家航空暨太空總署（NASA）錄製的宇宙聲響混合廟宇法會的聲音，更強化這種具有催眠的能量的無所不在，並且其中還隱藏著一般個人無法背叛的相互牽制力。

這裡碰觸的是與具地緣關係的宮廟組織緊密結合的過度稠密的鄰里社會關係網絡，回頭看《剖視島》中多元組合的開放異質關係，就碰觸到這類關係的調節的另一個關鍵問題。

●第二組：社會邊緣人藝術家自組具有影響力的關係網絡

1. 陳毅哲：《觀星者：2014-2020》

曾經是 921 大地震的受災戶，當時同樣遭遇災難的陌生人間建立親密連結及合作重建家園的事實，給藝術家重要的啟示。例如曾經運用淡水老街閒置多年的藥房經營為藝術替代空間，為了讓空間恢復能量，持續與不同社群合作與舉辦活動，後來再經營藝術空間，也循類似模式，在偶然的實際交遇與合作機會，透過拍攝以及建立簡單又質化的紀錄，建立一個可持續再交遇與合作的網絡。分散各處各行各業有相關能力的人何其多，如何將這些人連在一起做一點有趣有影響力的事情？這成為他的重要課題。

2. 鄧雯馨：《牆角窸窣囈語》

藝術家特別有機會進駐比較便宜、比較大、比較自由，但嚴重衰敗的房舍，在其中也較能體會必須與房子中不斷滋長的灰塵、壁癌、管線中的聲響等有機生命現象共生，甚至轉化為正面的創作能量。鄧雯馨借用這種關係來思考邊緣的藝術家與其生活居所或生存城市的共生關係：就有如病毒、黴菌、細菌般寄生在宿主身上，產生了相互影響的依附關係。2016 年於臺北景美跡岩成立「星空間」工作室，2 年後遷入台北當代藝術館旁安靜巷弄。她非常擅長藉由不同的藝術與創作活動，在工作室等空間串生無數的狂熱關係網絡。或反過來思考，她的藝術正是要透過串聯各種異質的能量去改變越來越均值的社會、越來越學院的藝術世界。

3. 林羿綺：《運行針：曼谷》

這是藝術家於泰國進行藝術創作駐村時的作品，她針對那些屬於城市邊緣地帶的異質場域進行一系列街頭游擊採訪，採集當地鬼魅與都市傳說等的親身經歷。敘事性的文字與深具寓意的城市影像畫面相互串聯映照之後，就如同被正在運行的針來回穿梭，逐漸拓展並打破敘事裡的空間，重新尋找鍵結，進行一場影像與城市空間的拓樸實驗。事實上，裡面的鬼魅故事和臺灣的靈異故事有高度的相似，這運行針不光運行在那幾個異國的邊緣地區，也運行在臺灣與泰國兩邊的邊緣地帶之間，她的很多作品都呈現這種的牽連。

4. 唐唐發 + FIDATI (PINDY WINDY)：《印尼雜貨店在台灣》

因應越來越多散居臺灣各地印尼移工和新住民的需求，城市及鄉間興起許多印尼雜貨店，這些雜貨店超越了商業交易行為的場所功能，成為了離鄉背井者維繫情感及延續文化傳統的聚集地。特別被安置在美術館中通道與服務空間旁邊的唐唐發與 FIDATI (PINDY WINDY) 的《印尼雜貨店在台灣》作品，其中所陳列看似一件件的商品，其實都是在臺印尼人所帶來與家鄉、家人連結的珍貴物品。有手工藝創作能力的印尼籍 FIDATI，在臺中東協廣場，定期帶領其他印尼同胞清理環境。原先我們希望她分享一些艱苦面，但她堅持要扭轉刻版印象，最後同意她的這個堅持，而成為真正的主題。兩位藝術家特別積極，在過程中啟動比其他作品更多的相關社群關係，例如臺灣的小孩與多年前照顧過她的家庭幫傭間不亞於親身父母的親情。

●第三組：以不同高度、速度運動及工作的物種

1. 鄧堯鴻：《繭影》、《剩餘與蔥翠》

《繭影》呈現的是腐爛得只剩半個身體的老鼠乾屍，假如《剩餘與蔥翠》呈現了倒閉餐廳的後台的不堪，那麼這件作品傳達的是困境中的頑強生命力。從牠殘破身軀剩下具有彈力的後腿及尾巴，看得出死前牠仍欲奔馳穿穴逾墙的強烈意志力。我們將這件作品擺在美術館最門面的入口處，並且透過兩邊巨大鏡面不斷反射，使得這隻到死還繼續努力奔跑尋找出口的老鼠，貫穿了整個美術館，傳達了這個展覽的核心關懷？

2. 黃彥超：《Food Winger》

隨時待命、騎摩托車執行外送熱食的工作，除了有每次的固定送餐費，也有尖峰或離峰時間的送餐累進獎金。例如四小時尖鋒時間中能送 14 次來計算，每小時會有 350 元！但你要為這個獎金制度賣命嗎？機車保養、油錢、甚至保險等等的支出全都是自費。只要在外面，就有機會颳風下雨曬太陽，還要確保餐點到達目的地，還要確保外送員自身的安全。藝術家從一個剛畢業作為一種過度性工作的熱食外送員的視角，表達對這種剝削性工作的無奈。這邊特別希望強調前台及後台的差異，一個可以展現個人身體爆發力的工作，一個可以自由安排個人工作時間的工作，很快就會回歸到時實際的被動的、未被保護的被剝削的狀態。

3. 許惠晴：《邊境漫遊》

透過準空姐的教育訓練過程，當過空姐的藝術家告訴我們所不知道的故事。在模擬機艙的教室中，準空姐先接受大庭廣眾下從身材、貼身衣物到制服穿著的檢查糾正，接著是各種例行的、特殊的及偶發的旅客服務的訓練。不管做什麼都需姿態優美面帶笑容。家裡的幫傭可以消極怠惰，偶而可以給主人一點臉色，空姐卻不可，這是多麼折騰人的壓抑？經常性的不正常作息及時差又是多麼不健康的生活方式？另一件作品是穿著空姐制服，曾經是空姐的藝術家的不斷嘔吐，這是對於各種身體折磨，及對於行為規範的無言抗議？空姐的這個工作，是最能突現前台與後台之間的劇烈差異的工作。

假如我們是那位暫時找不到固定工作的熱食外送員，假如我們是那位在天上到處飛以及為旅客服務的空中小姐，不久的將來還有開放民間超級昂貴的太空旅行，我們如何反思我們身體運動與城市的關係，以及特別是提供服務的個體們所擁有的主體性的問題？以及被服務者與服務者之間越來越大的懸殊？

●第四組：難以掙脫歷史迷障的回歸？

1. 梁廷毓：《襲奪之河》
藝術家透過歷史死亡地景，挖掘不同族群雙方深層記憶與泛靈宇宙相互交疊地域。其中〈圖誌〉呈現桃園大溪、龍潭、復興與新竹關西一帶，過去原、漢衝突頻繁的四方交界之處，因當地地形與地質條件觸發的死亡地景及過去地方歷史。〈脊谷〉與〈襲奪河〉從原、客族群雙方耆老的交叉敘事中，追溯昔日發生衝突的死亡地點、親族記憶、無頭鬼與石爺傳說。讓過往的死亡恐懼依舊徘徊縈繞在地方記憶與地景之中，形成了一個共享於族群雙方的深層記憶與泛靈宇宙相互交疊的地域。〈問石〉則特別說明地方誌的書寫包含非常重要的跨越人類主體的神靈視角。他的作品其實也讓我們思考，臺灣自古以來存在的族群衝突會不會持續進行？並且以不同的神話來醜化或美化。

2. 張徐展：《Si So Mi》
奇怪的標題《Si So Mi》，源自臺灣人對喪葬儀隊的稱呼，臺灣喪葬儀式本來就充滿各種矛盾現象，例如以「代哭」為表演活動的陣頭出現在莊嚴肅穆的喪禮中，希望吸引親朋好友的電子花車最後轉變為女性藝人表演的舞台，更有脫衣舞、鋼管女郎等的出現，使得真實與演出，悲哀嚴肅與歡慶荒誕界線非常模糊。當張徐展把被汽車壓扁令人厭惡又老又醜的死老鼠乾西樂儀隊與那隻可愛一臉無辜正在過生日的幼鼠放進這個脈絡，以及最後圍在四周像蛆一樣無聲無息環繞爬行的無名生物隊伍，是不是某種負責清理各種擾亂社會清潔及秩序的神秘組織，等整個極盡荒誕的死亡儀式及所有人證物證都清理完畢後，悄悄再從儀式廣場退回到森林中一間神秘陰森的宮廟，循環播出的影片加強了這類儀式的經常發生。

3. 顏忠賢：《地獄變相》
也是長篇小說家的顏忠賢說：「長篇小說永遠超負載的真實……就像是永遠無法逃離的『全員逃走中』被開地太過分太哭笑不得玩笑的巨大機關陣仗，或像是這裡痛那裡痛但仍然始終無法找到痛因的劫數的在劫難逃，或更像是某種被下咒太惡毒到這一世甚至永世不得超生的惡咒的永劫回歸……。」《地獄變相》不是民間宗教中的懲罰系統，對於這位有著奇特視角的跨界藝術家，人間太複雜必須透過扭曲變形的《地獄變相》架構，才足以交互重疊影射出其中的複雜性。地上被綑綁的那些還活著的大小肉塊，有些呻吟，有些好像在痛苦中仍然發出奇怪的笑聲，上面的殘酷的各種審判者才是被惡咒的對象？這些事情可能以不同程度發生在不同地方不同時代？我認為姚瑞中的《巨神連線》也可以放在這個脈絡之中。

4. 郭奕臣：《這是人類的一小步，物種的一大步》
確實和登月有關，有趣的是月球漫遊車主要部分竟然是飛機失事時讓飛行員能彈跳脫險的坐位。從側面看，月球漫遊車像一隻機器鳥，頭部是登月太空人用過的攝影機的相同機種，有趣的是椅背上還帶有恐龍特徵的始祖鳥圖案。從恐龍演化為鳥需要多少的時間？人類從鳥學習飛行，到脫離地心引力飛向太空抵達月球，卻在非常壓縮的時間中完成。人類透過工具發明突破本身先天的極限，也依據自身利益，改變其它物種的自然天性，長此以往，毫無節制超越極限的慾望,將要把人類及物種帶往怎樣的未來?其實他的問題可能是:為何我們要急著跟隨這種慾望潮流,而忽略更基本的生存需求?

5. 吳宜樺:《裡外急轉彎的 D 場景》

在重疊著已經風化的世界大戰古戰場以及充滿各種消費殘骸更新的荒地上,投影出人工智慧時代充滿各種爆炸火光的電腦虛擬戰爭遊戲的場景,好像在揭示不同世代不斷重複的錯誤。在這直接的理解上,還要追問《莉莉瑪蓮》這首反覆播放的反戰歌曲,瑪麗・瑪德蓮娜,德國演員兼歌手,《莉莉瑪蓮》正是她最有名的歌。在個人生活中她堅決反對德國的納粹政府,二戰期間她投身人道主義事業,為德國及法國避難和流亡者提供住所和經濟支持,並為其爭取美國公民權。反覆播放的《莉莉瑪蓮》,讓我們重新思考「叛國」這兩個字的超越國家的正面意涵。我們是否可以思考在不同時代生產不同的具有正面意義的「叛國」?

6. 郭俞平:《一盞燈進入房子,看不到其他房子》

這件作品和中興新村這個夢幻新市鎮有關,中興新村為過去中華民國臺灣省政府駐地所在,其整體都市設計參仿英國倫敦「新市鎮」創建模式而設計建造完成,並成為辦公與住宅合一的田園式行政社區。「凍省」對於在那安身立命的公務員,無疑是一個舒適、安穩的時代的結束。身為公務員子弟的藝術家郭俞平,卻透過這兩次的斷裂提出她非常尖銳的提問:人民對所依歸的烏托邦願景有無盡追尋,然而尚未落成就已擱置,成為廢墟。難道只有中興新村這個例子,臺灣會不會持續有這類最後以殘局落幕的烏托邦願景?

Re-visiting *Perforated City*

Text | Hai-Ming Huang

An exhibition cannot stop on the day of its opening. It is very important to re-think the overall exhibition with a certain distance despite the fact that it is a very tiring task to re-start at a trying moment!

● Foreword

Perforation is related to the inevitable deterioration of hardware; however, the core curatorial interest of *Perforated City* has been the existential experiences of individuals or groups when traversing different mediums. This surely denotes a complicated relationship and process that include different environments, times, myths, classes, rates and obstructions, in which different individuals or groups are actively or passively rising, sinking, numbed, awakened, progressing while evolving, collapsing while moving, or suffering frustration while trying get back on their feet. Sometimes they disperse and connect in disparate ways; and at other times, they encounter dissimilar formation, separation or obstruction. In simple words, the perforated city or perforated town is a platform as well as a medium that reveals a wide range of relations.

This essay will develop and organize the relationships that we have individually developed while observing their interrelations at all times through four independent yet interrelated aspects. The museum, at first, defined this exhibition as a way to think about space, and we mainly focused on the complicated network related to causality, time and space that concerns the lower social stratum. Furthermore, regarding the initial curatorial process, more new questions have now emerged.

● Group 1: Fixation, Split and Entanglement of Social Relations and Networks

1.Chen Po-I: *Yin Yang Huajiang—Wandering Scenes of the Collective Housing*

This area was previously a traditional agricultural community by the river that consisted of houses, farms and vegetable patches. Later, roads that appeared after regional and comprehensive urban and rural development – in particular, elevated transportation systems comprising expressways and land bridges – forcibly severed the intimately linked neighborhood. Huajiang House, incorporated with highly creative circular overpasses and corridors, to a certain extent, protects the communal relationship between individuals as well as people and the environment. The artist utilizes a special artistic approach to bring forth the previous bonding, communal charm formed by the outdoor potted plants in the corridors shared by the households and the shared, interweaving indoor and outdoor spaces in the dilapidated, lonely Huajiang House.

2.Yu-Hao Hung: *Wanderland*

In the dark exhibition space, this work creates a scene of intertwining alleyways found in old neighborhoods, producing a feeling of an intimate labyrinth, as if one might accidentally wander into a neighbor's private space. The artist also makes use of two backlit doors in the exhibition space and artist Chen Po-I's rather transparent images featuring corridors in the museum hallway to convert this part of the museum into a space that blurs the distinction between public and private spaces. The artist is especially good at combining typical storefront overhang, installation comprising everyday objects and videos to gradually deconstruct the originally closely connected living space, which, after its deconstruction, could look desolate and strange to those that occasionally wander back to the space.

3.Chu ChunTeng: *August 15th*

This work begins with an incident about a dementia patient, who has wandered off from the nursing home and gotten lost since the date of *August 15th*. One of the figures in the videos is an old woman, who keeps wandering around due to her dementia caused by the Alzheimer's disease. According to the artist, "during the year of preparing this work, I intensively contacted friends with memory issues and cognitive dislocation and their family members...However, as time passed, I started to see myself, and realized that the so-called 'symptomatic memory loss' is something that happens to us every day." Around or inside modern communities, many people have in fact lived in their own parallel worlds. While the first two works speak about the collapsing of communities resulting from the development of society, *August 15th* portrays how people, despite their physical nearness, live in different and parallel worlds because of aging, illnesses, dementia or many other internal factors.

4.Eric Chen: *Section Assembly Island*

The artist and I discussed about an idea—"a cross section of an old apartment would be the most fascinating theater." This idea has something to do with his previous work, *The Landscape of the Boundary*, made with bamboo scaffolding. Coming from the background of architecture, Chen nevertheless does not focus on old apartments; neither does he try to highlight the nostalgic sentiments they embody. Instead, he casts his eye to shared inhabitation and sensibility in the future society. According to the artist, "the various sections of apartments create many holes that allow interconnections between different positions, engendering new possibilities." After an elaborate, thorough process of communication and adjustment, *Section Assembly Island*, a title that marks a grand scale, eventually adopts an open structure, and ingeniously amalgamates Kuo I-Chen's work that reflects on the compulsivity of technology and Chu Chun-Teng's work that contemplates on the phenomenon of parallel worlds while generating intriguing dialogues with Wu Yi-Hua's and Kuo Yu-Ping's highly critical works as well as Deng Yau-Horng's enormous, desiccated rat below the second-floor ground.

5.YAO Jui-Chung: *Incarnation*

Through gigantic deity statues born from the projection of religious believers' "powerful drives" from around Taiwan, the artist constructs the intricately interwoven tapestry of people's life, the culture of folk religions and politico-economic relations within the geographic borders of Taiwan. The artist emphasizes on the photographic viewpoint in the work, attempting to capture people's state of shock when suddenly seeing the extraordinarily large deity statues as they walk on the streets. Furthermore, the three-channel projection has rendered the images more impactful. In this case, I believe that the use of sound is equally crucial: the mixture of high-volume cosmic sounds recorded by the National Aeronautics and Space Administration (NASA) and the sounds of religious temple fairs even reinforces this hypnotic energy that seems omnipresent, with mutually restraining forces that individuals cannot betray.

This work touches upon the network of social relations based on overly dense neighborhoods that are closely combined with religious temples with geographical vicinity. Looking back on *Section Assembly Island*, the open, heterogeneous relations of diverse combinations in the work also touches upon another key issue regarding the adjustment of such relations.

● Group 2: The Influential Relationship Network Formed by Socially Marginal Artists

1.Yi-Che, Chen: *Stargazing: 2014-2020*

Once a victim in the 1999 Jiji Earthquake, the artist had an important epiphany after witnessing strangers that were also victims formed a close relationship and collaborated to rebuild their homes. He therefore converted a drug store that was vacant for many years on the old street of Tamsui into an alternative art space. In order to revitalize the space, they continued working with different communities and organizing events. Later, he also followed a similar pattern to run other art spaces—through random but real encounters and opportunities of collaboration, he has created a network of sustainable encounters and collaborations through photographing and establishing simple and qualitative records. There are countless people with different abilities from all walks of life. How to bring these people together to do things that are fun and can generate an impact becomes a major topic for him.

2.Teng Wen-Hsin: *Murmur and Whisper*

The artist had a chance to move into a cheaper, larger space with more freedom. The downside was that the house itself was in a terribly deteriorating condition. In the house, the artist became aware that she had to share the space with phenomena that resembled organic life forms, such as dust, efflorescence and noisy pipelines in the house; she even turned such a condition into positive creative energies. Teng Wen-Hsin tried to reflect on a marginal artist's symbiotic relationship with his or her residence or city through her personal relationship with her house—it was like how viruses, fungi and bacteria depend and live off of their hosts, creating mutual influences. In 2016, she founded Hsin'Space at Xianjiyan in Jingmei, Taipei, and moved to a quiet alley next to MOCA Taipei two years later. She specializes in weaving countless zealous networks together through presenting different artistic and creative events at her studio. In a way, her art has been to bring different heterogeneous energies together to change the increasingly homogenizing society and the art world that is becoming more and more academic.

3.LIN, Yi-Chi: *Running Stitch – Bangkok*

This work was created during the artist's residency in Thailand. In a guerilla style, she interviewed people on the streets in heterogeneous sites in the city's peripheral regions, and gathered personal experiences relating to local supernational tales and urban myths. The descriptive text and the profoundly metaphorical images of the city are strung together and mirror each other in a way that is similar to a running stitch, gradually expanding as well as shattering the space in the narratives while forming new links in this topographical experiment of image and urban space. In fact, some of the gathered supernatural stories and the ghost stories in Taiwan share great similarities. This running stitch not only operates in the peripheral regions in the foreign country but also in the peripheral regions of both Taiwan and Thailand. Many of Lin's works have demonstrated such connection.

4.Tang Tang-Fa + FIDATI (PINDY WINDY): *Indonesian Grocery Store in Taiwan*

To cope with the needs of increasing migrant workers and new residents from Indonesia that are living around Taiwan, more and more Indonesian grocery stores have emerged in cities and the countryside. These grocery stores exceed their functionality as sites of commercial activities and have become gathering hubs for the expatriates to stay connected and continue their cultural tradition. Indonesian Grocery Store in Taiwan by Tang Tang-Fa and FIDATI (PINDY WINDY) is specially placed in the hallway next to the museum's service area. The items displayed in the installation are in reality precious objects brought by the Indonesians in Taiwan that connect them to their homes and families. Indonesian artist FIDATI, who creates handcrafts, regularly leads her fellow countrymen to clean the environment of Taichung's ASEAN Square. Originally, we had hoped that she could share some of her bitter experiences with the audience. However, she insisted that such a stereotypical impression had to be overturned, and we eventually reached a consensus and turned her idea into the theme of the work. The two artists have been particularly active and set in motion more related communal relations during the creative process than other artists have done in other works; for instance, one could see a Taiwanese girl's relationship with a domestic worker that had looked after her, which is no less stronger than her relationship with her parents.

● Group 3: Varied Species Moving and Working at Different Altitude and Speed

1.Deng Yau-Horng: *Shadow of a Cocoon* **and** *Remainder and Green*

Shadow of a Cocoon shows half of a rat's rotten, desiccated body. Whereas *Remainder and Green* portrays the embarrassing reality of behind the counter in a bankrupt restaurant, *Shadow of a Cocoon* contrarily signals a resilient life force in a difficult situation. Judging from the rat's brawny hind legs and tail on what is left on its half-broken body, one can see its strong will as if it were still trying to run through the wall when it died. We place this work at the entrance of the museum as the first piece in the exhibition and employ the endless mirror reflection in two large mirror walls on both sides. In this way, the rat that strove to find an exit before it died has penetrated the entire museum, conveying the core concern of the exhibition.

2.Huang Yen-Chao: *Food Winger*

Always standing by on scooters to deliver food straight from restaurant kitchens, food deliverers not only receive regular delivery fees every time a task is successfully performed but also bonus fees for delivering at specific peak and off-peak periods. For example, during the four hours of the peak period, if a deliverer could complete fourteen deliveries, he or she could earn $350 per hour. However, do you want to slave for this bonus-earning system? Scooter maintenance, gas and even insurance are all out of the deliverers' own pockets. As long as they are outdoors, they might have to endure fierce wind, rain and sunlight while having to make sure that the meals are delivered on time as well as their personal safety. The artist adopts the perspective of a food deliverer, who has taken such a transitional job as a new graduate, and expresses the helplessness in these exploitative occupations. I specially hope to emphasize the difference between the front end and the back end—a job that demonstrates an individual's physical explosive power and allows one to freely schedule the working hours may quickly fall back into the state of exploitation that in reality puts one in a passive and unprotected position.

3.HSU, HUI-CHING: *Border Roaming*

By showing the educational training for flight attendants, the artist, who used to be a flight attendant herself, reveals stories that we normally would not know. In a mock cabin that serves as a classroom, a would-be flight attendant must be examined for appearance and corrected in terms of her figure, undergarments and how she wears the uniform. The check-up is followed by a wide range of trainings to meet the routine, special and unordinary services required by passengers. No matter what she does, she must maintain a pleasant look with an endearing smile. While a domestic worker might sometimes be passive and lazy, expressing an unpleasant attitude to his or her employer, a flight attendant can never do so. How torturingly suppressive is this job! The frequently irregular daily schedule and the time differences also create a highly unhealthy lifestyle. In another work, the artist resumed her previous role as a flight attendant, putting on the uniform and continuously vomiting. Is it a silent protest against the extent of physical torments and the behavioral restraints? The occupation of flight attendant can most clearly highlight the drastic differences between the front end and the back end.

If we were the food deliverer who could not find a steady job for the time being, or the flight attendant that would fly from one place to another and serve passengers in the air – especially when excessively expensive space travels will be available for the private sector – how do we think about the relationship between our physical movement and a city, particularly the subjectivity of individuals that provide services, along with the growing disparity between those serving and those served?

● Group 4: Returning to the Inescapable Haze of History?

1.Liang Ting-Yu: *The Capturing River*
The artist uses historically ominous landscape to explore the region where deep memories of different ethnic communities and the pantheist universe overlap. *Cartography: Mutu* features local history and ominous landscape, deadly due to the topographical and geological reality, in the intersecting borders among Taoyuan's Daxi, Longtan, Fuxing and Hsinchu's Guanxi, where conflicts between the indigenous community and the Han people frequently occurred in the past. *The Ridge and the Valley* and *Blood Flows in Rivers* trace the locations of deadly conflicts in the past, family memories, the legend of ghouls and "Shiye" (literally, "stone father") through the interweaving narratives of elders from the indigenous and Hakka communities. The past fear of death still seem to haunt and linger in memories of the place and the landscape, producing a region shared by both communities and characterized by the tapestry of deep memories and the pantheist universe. *The Cartography of Stone*, on the other hand, specifically points

out that the writing of chorography includes a crucial supernature perspective that surpasses the human subject. Liang's works, in fact, enable us to think about whether the long-lasting ethnic conflicts in Taiwan would continue and be vilified or glorified with different myths.

2.ZHANG XU zhan: *Si So Mi*

The curious title, *Si So Mi*, originates from the nickname of traditional Taiwanese funeral procession band. Traditional Taiwanese funeral is itself a mélange of contradictory phenomena, for instance, the performative "substitute mourners" (also known as professional mourners) in supposedly solemn, serious funerals; the electric flower cars that are originally meant for attracting friends and relatives and later turned into stages for female entertainers; and the appearance of strip dancing and pole dancers. These elements blur the distinction between realty and performance as well as gloomily tearful funerals and joyfully festive celebrations. Zhang combines this context with a marching band comprising disgusting, unpleasant-looking, desiccated rats crushed by cars and an innocent-looking rat pup celebrating its birthday, together with a pack of nameless, silently crawling, maggot-like creatures around them. They seem like some unknown organization that is in charge of tidying up different disturbances that mess up the cleanliness and order of the society. After the extremely absurd ritual of death is performed and all the evidence cleaned up, they then quietly retreat from the square of the ritual into some mysterious, dim temple in the forest. The looping of the video strongly implies that this type of rituals have often taken place.

3.Yan Chung-Hsien: *Hell*

Artist Yan Chung-Hsien is also a novelist. According to him, "novel is a reality that is always overloaded···like a vast, inescapable array of apparatuses with over-the-top, exceedingly awkward jokes in the movie, *Run for Money*; or like a fateful doom cursed with inexplainable pain, of which the reason can never be found; or even the eternal damnation from some curses that persist through a lifetime or last through eternity." *Hell* does not show a system of punishment common in folk religions. For this interdisciplinary artist who adopts a special point of view, the world is so complicated that its complexity can only be projected through the interlapping structure of the distorted, transmogrified *Hell*. Some of the bound, living lumps of meat in various sizes on the floor seem to be moaning; and some seem to be making weird laughing sounds in their agonizing state. Or, could it be that the cruel judges in their different looks the cursed ones? Could these things, in different degrees, be happening at different places in different times? I believe that Yao Jui-Chung's *Incarnation* can also be placed in this context.

4.KUO I-Chen: *That's One Small Step for Mankind, One Giant Leap for Species*

This work is indeed related to moon landing. Interestingly, a main component of this lunar roving vehicle is the ejector seat that allows an aircraft pilot to escape life-threatening danger. From its side, the lunar roving vehicle looks like a robotic bird, and its top is installed with the same model of camera used by astronauts in the mission of moon landing. The back of the chair intriguingly carries the symbol of an dinosaur-like Archaeopteryx. How long did it take for dinosaurs to evolve into birds? Human beings, from imitating flying birds to being able to escape gravity and land on the moon, however, only spent a very condensed, relatively short period of time. Through inventing instruments, human beings have defied natural limitations and also altered other species' nature according to our own interest. Over the course of history, we have unrestrainedly surpassed the limit of desire. What kind of a future are human beings creating for ourselves and other species? What the artist is trying to ask is perhaps this: why are we so desperate to follow our desires and ignore the fundamental needs for survival?

5.WU Yi-Hua: *Inside-out D-scène*

On the overlapping layers of a weathered battleground of ancient world wars and a wasteland filled with remnants of consumer products, the video projection reveals a a computerized, virtual war game characterized by varied scenes of explosions in this era of artificial intelligence, signaling the mistakes that have been repeated by every generation. With this direct understanding, we can also ask about the anti-war song, entitled "Lili Marleen," used in this work. "Lili Marleen" is the most well-known song by German singer-actress, Marie Magdalene (widely known as Marlene Dietrich). In real life, she was a resolute dissenter against the Nazi government, and during WWII, she also dedicated her time to humanitarian works, providing accommodation and financial support for German and French refugees and exiles while fighting hard to get them American citizenship. Repeatedly playing "Lili Marlene" encourages us to reconsider a potentially positive meaning of the notion of "treason" that transcends the concept of nation. Could we think about other positive meanings of "treason" produced in different eras?

6.Kuo Yu-Ping: *There Is a Light That Enters Houses With No Other House In Sight*

This work is related to an idealized new community that is known as Zhongxing New Village, which used to be where the Provincial Government of Taiwan, R.O.C. was located. Its overall planning imitated the layout and design of London's new town, and became a rural administrative district that combined office buildings and residential housing. The "streamlining and nationalization of the provincial government," for the public servants that had considered their careers secured, was undoubtedly the end of a comfortable, stable era. However, the artist, having parents that were public servants, poses a rather sharp question through the two breaks: people had endlessly pursued the utopian vision that gave them a sense of belonging. However, the pursuit was never accomplished and what was left were mere ruins. Could there be more examples in Taiwan like that of Zhongxing New Village, where similar utopian visions have eventually ended up as unfulfilled dreams?

Essays

專文　　⊘

失落的地龍國：一座穿孔中的城市憂鬱

文｜高千惠

我碰到好多人，駝著背向前行走。他們每個人的背上都背著個巨大的怪物 (幻想)，其
重量猶如一袋麵粉，一袋煤或是羅馬步兵的行裝。可是，這怪物並不是一件僵死的重
物，相反，它用有力的，帶彈性的肌肉把人緊緊地摟壓著，用它兩隻巨大的前爪勾住背
負著的胸膛，並把異乎尋常的大腦袋壓在人的額頭上，就像古時武士們用來威嚇敵人而
戴在頭上的可怕的頭盔。

——波特萊爾《巴黎的憂鬱》

1.

波特萊爾在《巴黎的憂鬱》散文集裡，揭開了 19 世紀的天龍國—巴黎，那個與華麗、光鮮
表象相反的另一面—骯髒、畸形中的地下社會。他以「街頭巷尾」的觀察與「奇篇怪章」的
書寫，呈現了一座城市的負面空間。這個負面空間是過去與現在擠壓出的縫隙之域，具有
「惡之華」般的陰黯魅力。它是現代城市的角落陰影，以地下道之姿統御著幽暗的現實空間，
成為歡樂城市看不見的憂鬱。英國奇幻小說《哈利波特》，則以倫敦英王十字車站為現實場
景，虛構出一個能穿越到魔幻世界的九又四分之三月台。每年霍格沃茨特快列車，將自此開
出。而只有巫師們，才能從這個隱匿的月台，撞進另一個常眼看不見的異世界。

2020 年春，以台北當代藝術館作為「九又四分之三月台」，黃海鳴、黃香凝偕同策展的「大
加蚋堡憂鬱」，透過藝術家們介於現實與魔幻的想像，共築出一個有關失落與成長中的「穿孔
城市」。[1] 藝術家鄧堯鴻在入口形象區與廊道出現的《繭影》，正是以陰暗、腐敗、剩殘的巨
大怪物之屍、渺小脆弱的鼠屍之形，作為此展的主意象，進而打開城市裡的慾望地窖，暴露
出那些寄於神鬼的、靈異的、邊緣的、迷惘的、脫節的、與前進時代相背卻又頑強存在的現
實社會。如其《剩餘與蒼翠》中的剩餘與廢棄物，所有的殘餘與殘缺，都是完整前的參與者，
與完整後的被拋棄者。它們以另一種形態存在，在不完整與不確定中，展開另類的生命力。

《穿孔城市》一展，其英譯採用了「Perforated City」。這個術語原來自 2006 年，約翰 · 耶
森 (Johann Jessen) 發表在《德國城市研究》雜誌，一篇有關都更的文章。約翰 · 耶森在文
章中提述：東德城市花了好幾年時間，才能夠接受萎縮的事實。在此知覺障礙下，萊比錫是
首批克服集體自欺，重拾鐵鍬，面對「穿孔城市」的狀態，而有了管理其收縮局勢的行動。[2]

2010 年，城鄉研究者丹尼 · 弗羅倫汀 (Daniel Florentin) 在〈穿孔城市：萊比錫的城市收
縮管理模式〉(Perforated City: Leipzig's Model of Urban Shrinkage Management) 論文中，即
採用「穿孔城市」一詞作命題，以此描述德國萊比錫的都更計劃之前提。[3] 在原意上，「穿

孔城市」在於描述一個新時代，其特徵是人口下降和城市蔓延的同時出現，致使城市面臨異化狀態。弗羅倫汀的案例研究為經驗研究，包括介入者的訪談以及對統計數據的分析。而其結論是，如神祕瑪雅人的面紗，萊比錫的城市策略可能是一個誘餌，旨在掩蓋缺乏影響力和財務實力下，試圖實現其管控城市萎縮的目的。[4]

以舊稱「大加蚋堡」的臺北為在地現代化的擴張核心，當代藝術館的「穿孔城市」，選擇從步登公寓建築體出發。這些源自 1920 年代的現代主義社會住宅，在 1960 年代至 1970 年代間，以四、五層雙拼梯間型的集合住宅形態，出現於臺北，成為這個被當代臺灣稱為「天龍國」之摩登生活空間雛型。[5]進入 1990 年代，在大廈叢林拔地而起中，它們已逐漸長出一塊興衰交接的黑影，收納著庶民無法割拾的日常，以及一些從未趕上現代化失速列車的拋棄物與剩餘物。

這個被譽為「天龍國」的城市空間，散發著過去的、與正發生的新進異味。此平行時空般地存在的黯黑「地龍國」，不是榮耀的城市景觀，不是引以為傲的地方性。但它卻成為養育藝術家與文學家們的靈感，這些靈感以怪奇物語的聊齋形式呈現。在幾分真實與幾分虛構中，穿孔出城市中的多維世界。

2.
從藝術家們所呈現的城市角落景觀，認識一座城市獨特的憂鬱，足以還原出一種與歷史經驗有關的地方性。這些地方藝術家似乎都長了島嶼居民特有的「陰陽眼」，樂於同步地呈現出二個並置而又顛倒的世界。此「穿孔城市」的非物質性、具量子糾纏般的「鬼故事」，選擇以人間陽宅的幽幽腸徑、地府陰宅的爍爍神明、邊緣性與滲透性的殖性場域，如八孔嗩吶的鳴放，展演了一個異質空間並存的劇場。

人間居所的幽幽腸徑，是身體與空間最密切的穿梭與留佇場域。興於 1960 年代的步登公寓，成為未終結的記憶空間，無法被棄置，也無法再前進。剩下的便是幻覺與幻境，以確切被相信的存在，漫遊在實境裡。陳伯義的《步移景換・華江陰陽》，以攝影的光影技法，與建築師陳其寬畫作《陰陽》對話，其無人的場景，呈現了 1970 年代華江集合住宅的公共性與私密性。洪譽豪的《無以為家》，則選擇以 3D 掃描，紀錄了臺北舊城區的萬華一帶騎樓，與附生出的常民生活樣態。這些商居共生的騎樓，多已成為攤販、地攤、遊民、過客、住民川流與交融的生活場域，似家又非家，形成了活的時間膠囊。

從遠古到未來，物種的演化是物競天擇，還是科技使然？在尋找天外天的行動中，更好的物種，能否應允更美好的未來？在進化與退化之間，那個登月年代的生活空間，喻指了劇烈加速度的科技進擊，正如同巨大的怪物前爪，勾住擁抱過去的胸膛。在核心展域中，陳宣誠的《剖視島》，以「步登公寓」為原型，打造了一個層層疊疊的木作建物劇場。如一個有生命的鴿舍空間，它承載了建築體與人際之間的關係，也坦露鴿籠內的有限視界。在這個小木作島上，除了失去時間感的記憶檔案，也飄浮者古早的未來展望氣息。

《剖視島》的鷹架一側，是朱駿騰的《八月十五》，那是記憶與認知錯位者所行走的迴旋空間，屬於時間停滯、失去、尋找的狀態。鷹架一端是郭奕臣對登月年代的科幻想像作品《這是人類的一小步，物種的一大步》，以並不前端的科技裝置，提出狩獵未來的跨時空想望。另外一隅，郭俞平的《一盞燈進入房子，看不到其他房子》，則以多重的錄像、聲音與物件，作了似乎在裝修，又仿若被棄置的空間裝置。三部影片企圖說出冷戰時期，那個透過現代化而不斷建設中的年代慾望，以及有關一些被打碎的、被重組的破壞與建構。吳宜樺的《裡外急轉彎的D場景》，則將熟悉的日常物件與生活場景，作了詩性與機械性的肢解與異位。[6] 藉著影像幻術、異質物件錯位等部署，此場景提出人工智慧時代氾濫的合成影像景觀，已將人引入一個由失序與約制並構的人類世烏托邦裡。

除了群體的世界，個人的居所也是想望的起源地。藝術，多產於波希米亞式的生活空間。鄧雯馨的《牆角窸窣囈語》，以藝術家 2016 年間，在臺北景美仙跡岩成立的工作室，以及 2 年後遷入台北當代藝術館旁的安靜巷弄為再現景觀。藉由不同的創作活動，藝術家在城市角落，如菌般地寄生於宿主，也串生了無數共生的關係網絡。陳毅哲的《觀星者》，則是藝術家於 2014 年到 2016 年，進駐淡水老街的閒置空間。在該寄宿地，藝術家為了使廢棄空間恢復生活機能，同樣與不同的社群合作，建立了藝術工作上的人際臉譜。這兩組作品，都涉及了由過去的實體空間，延展出未來的人際空間。

3.

白日退去，黑夜復來。陰宅的燦燦神明，在多元信仰的人世間，成為在場空間的另類見証者。梁廷毓影像裝置的《襲奪之河》，地景所在是桃園大溪、龍潭、復興與新竹關西一帶，也是過去原、漢衝突頻繁的的交界之處。[7] 在原、客族群耆老們的交叉敘事中，昔日發生衝突的死亡地點、部族記憶、民間傳奇、靈異經驗，形成族群雙方的深層記憶，以及與泛靈世界交疊的人文空間。顏忠賢的《地獄變相》，則據其小說文本，以軟物質紮裹出漢民信仰中的閻王殿景觀，現覺化臺灣民間傳說中的地府遊記。張徐展的《Si So Mi》，則以喪葬儀隊的儀式與常被使用的西樂隊歌曲，紙紮的鼠輩世界，再現一個屬於亡靈的狂歡景象。

漢、原民的靈異空間、鄉野鬼魅與都市傳說交結的異質場域非現實疆域，在當代東南亞交流活動裡，成為跨域共享的非物質文明。林羿綺的《運行針：曼谷》，是藝術家於泰國駐村時的作品。藝術家在泰國曼谷地區街頭，進行游擊式採訪，以三個不同區域的超自然經驗作為串連，有了「我在這裡沒有遇到靈魂，但是我有我的故事要說。」的開場白。臺灣南北出現的巨大神像景觀，再次証明臺灣的生活空間，具有人神鬼共存的地理體質。姚瑞中的《巨神連線》，即拍攝了全臺各地一尊尊大規模的巨大神像，共構出臺灣地理空間內的常民生活、信仰文化與政治經濟之交錯關係。藝術家透過三頻道錄像、美國太空總署（NASA）錄製的宇宙聲響與廟宇法會之混合聲，以梵梵之音共振出這個奇觀社會。

4.

邊緣性、服務性的場域，同樣連結出「工具化」的身體與空間關係。許惠晴的《邊境漫遊》，以其曾任空服員的角色，在機艙空間裡，變換出不同的服務身份。影片中空姐，在客艙中因應旅客的提供物，主動與被動地變裝，呈現出多視角下的身體景觀。黃彥超的《Food Winger》，來自「行動送餐」這個興起的新型態消費模式。藝術家將外送員每日移動的路徑—介入街道地圖的日常繞圈行為，視為城市的新人文地理圖式，同時也喻指了工具化人生的形成。

潛入的「殖性」，逐漸改變消費世界的景觀。唐唐發的《印尼雜貨店在台灣》，以在臺印尼人與家鄉連結的物品陳列，提出了東南亞新移民的物質世界與消費文化。這些外來生活文化物件的介入，滲透出臺灣街頭景觀必然會轉變。被稱為「在地地」的景觀，將集合了過去的「地方性」，以及穿孔中的「新地方性」。它們不再是廢墟或殘餘物，而是有些熟悉、有些陌生的異味與添加物。

每一個城市的穿孔故事都有其地方性。新移民生活文化的滲入，在人口上、經濟上、文化上，未必經過硬體空間更換的城市易容，同樣也會出現一種「在地性與殖性」的流變現象，以便延續其既是千瘡百孔，又是無孔不入的狀態。繁華的天龍國或許在膨脹，或許在萎縮。這種穿孔作用，既發生在實體建物，也發生在社群人際關係上。「Ruin」一詞，遂以侵蝕性的動詞狀態與形成實體的名詞型態，築構出城市的身體景觀，也提供了一種「天人五衰」般的警世之象。[8]

在全球化的城市競爭中，所有穿孔中的城市，並非只有各別的「廢墟故事」，它還包括了科技文明與遷移人口帶來的矛盾「殖性」。以「穿孔城市」，作為臺灣現代化過程中的城市比喻，「穿孔」一詞，似乎被視為一種穿透、敗壞的象徵。陳述故事的藝術家們，或在明處，或在暗處；或許早已存在，或許被召集而來。這些作品，像一首首在現代性的徘徊中，由藝術家們的「在場」與「缺席」，所共譜出的陰翳之詩，展示了一個看得見與看不見的「失落中的地龍國」。

如是我觀。如果「巴黎的憂鬱」是以孤獨城市的漫遊者之眼，佐以文字，調動一座城市的幽靈；那麼，此「大加蚋堡的憂鬱」，則是試圖以集眾的視覺景觀，召喚出一座城市的幽靈，誦出了一個人鬼神共處的社會風景線。這個空間，是現實，也是奇觀，並在連結中，產生一種無法複製的生命力。

[1] 「大加蚋」傳為平埔族語 Ketagalan（凱達格蘭）之語，類似音 Tagal 有「沼澤」之意。大加蚋的範圍原以老臺北市萬華區新店溪沿岸一帶的平原。18 世紀初因成為漢人聚落，其範圍亦日漸增大，大加蚋改稱「大加蚋堡」。清同治年間，大加蚋堡的範圍已含括今日的臺北市與新北市等老區。日治時期，於 1920 年廢大加蚋堡，大加蚋之名遂淡出記憶。此文以「大加蚋堡的憂鬱」為以臺灣北部現代化空間發展作為隱喻，意指「天龍國」誕生之前與誕生之後，一個集體記憶與集體失憶的隱藏居住空間。

[2] 約翰・耶森（Johann Jessen）原文發表於 2006 年。本資料參閱丹尼・弗羅倫汀（Daniel Florentin）的〈穿孔城市：萊比錫的城市收縮管理模式〉（Perforated City: Leipzig's Model of Urban Shrinkage Management），Berkeley Planning Journal（Volume 23, 2010）線上來源：https://escholarship.org/uc/item/97p1p1jx（2020/07/05）

[3] 自 1966 年以來，德國萊比錫即不斷處於城市的萎縮中。自 1989 年以來，在社會主義轉型下，才試圖轉變此現象。不同於德勒斯登等其他東德城市，萊比錫較早期適應了收縮和穿孔的局勢，嘗試管控城市的收縮，同時也利用此變化維持城市的形象。

[4] 據丹尼・弗羅倫汀（Daniel Florentin）研究，在萊比錫的規劃策略中，其三個主要軸是：保護具城市標地的建築遺產，創造綠色空間和開放空間以代替破舊住宅，建立中心的微觀等級體系。而在都更過程中，可預期地出現土地競爭和社會兩極分化的現象。

[5] 天龍人，是臺灣的網路流行用語。原詞來自日本漫畫《航海王》，為特權階級者的名稱，之後被引伸為臺灣一些長期或永久定居臺北市，不知人間疾苦的民眾。「天龍國」成為最現代化的臺北城市別名，並因地產房價與建物新型制，而有「天龍區」與「天龍城」的經濟階級之分。

[6] 藝術家在自述中，提出是以德國劇作家海納・穆勒（Heiner Müller）的《哈姆雷特機器》作為構思的靈感藍圖。參見館方展覽資料。

[7] 參見展覽現場中的文獻資料。

[8] 天人五衰，佛家語，意指天界的天人在壽命將盡時，所出現的種種現象。五衰又有大五衰、小五衰兩種。大五衰的天人將會墮入輪迴，小五衰的天人若遇到善根修行佛法，或者會有轉機。

The Lost Earthly Dragon Kingdom: The Melancholy of a Perforated City

Text | Chien-Hui KAO

I came upon a number of men who walked along bent over. Each of them carried on his back an enormous Chimera, heavy as a sack of flour or coal, or the backpack of a Roman foot soldier. But the monstrous beast was not an inert weight; on the contrary, it surrounded and oppressed the man with its elastic and powerful muscles; with its two great claws it clasped the chest of its mount; and its mythical head rose up over the man's head, like one of those horrific helmets that ancient warriors hoped would increase the enemy's sense of terror.

Baudelaire, *Le Spleen de Paris*

1.

Baudelaire unveiled the 19th century "Celestial Dragon Kingdom", Paris, in his prose poems collection *Le Spleen de Paris*. Beneath its glamourous and glorious appearance was the dirty and deformed underground society. He presented the city's negative space with the observation of "streets and lanes" and the writing of "bizarre chapters." This negative space was a realm of squeezed gaps between the past and the present, with a gloomy charm as the "Les Fleurs du mal." Like an underpass ruling the dark space in reality, the modern city's shady corners become an invisible melancholy in a joyous city. The British fantasy novel *Harry Potter* takes London King's Cross Railway Station as a real-life setting, creating the fictional Platform Nine and Three-Quarters that can travel to the magical world, where Hogwarts Express departs every year. Only wizards can crash into another world invisible to Muggle's eyes from this hidden platform.

In the spring of 2020, Hai-Ming Huang and Anita Hsiang-Ning Huang employed MOCA Taipei as the Platform Nine and Three-Quarters and curated "Le Spleen de Tuā-ka-lak-pó,"[1] constructing a "Perforated City" with artists' imagination betwixt reality and fantasy. Deng Yau-Horng's *Shadow of a Cocoon* is installed at the entrance and the hallway. This gloomy, decayed, incomplete monstrous carcass of the shape of a small, fragile rat is precisely the main imagery of this exhibition, aiming to open the vaults of desire in the city, unveiling the actual society that is spiritual, supernatural, marginal, lost, disconnected, and rebel to the progress of time but stubbornly existed. Just as the leftover items and scraps in the artist's *Remainder and Green*, all the residues and fragments were participants before completing the purpose and the abandoned after the achievement. They exist in another state which is incomplete and uncertain and take on an alternative vitality.

The English translation of this exhibition is *Perforated City*, which is originated from the article about urban planning by Johann Jessen published in the *German Journal of Urban Studies* in 2006. Jessen mentioned that it took Eastern German cities many years before they finally accepted the reality that they have shrunk. Among such disorders of perception, Leipzig was the first city to overcome collective self-deception and get back on track to confront the situation of a "perforated city," taking actions to administrate the shrinking.[2]

In 2010, Daniel Florentin published *Perforated City: Leipzig's Model of Urban Shrinkage Management*, in which he assigned "perforated city" as a topic to describe the reason for Leipzig's urban regeneration.[3] Initially, "perforated city" is a term to define a new era when population decline and urban sprawl co-occur, which lead to urban alienation. Florentin's case study was empirical research, including people who involve in management and statistical data analysis. His conclusion was that Leipzig's urban strategies were probably only decoys, as the Maya peoples' mysterious veil, aiming to conceal the fact the government lacked influence and financial strengths and attempted to manage the shrinkage.[4]

Taipei, used to be called Tuā-ka-lak-pó, was at the core of Taiwan's modernization. MOCA Taipei's "Perforated City" takes the walkup apartment as its starting point. Originated from the modernism council house in the 1920s, four or five stories walkup apartments that are paired with stairs emerged in Taipei during the 1960s to the 1970s. They have become the prototype of modern life of the "Celestial Dragon Kingdom," as how today's Taiwanese people call the city.[5] As the 1990s arrived, among the erection of the forest of apartment buildings, walkup apartments have shrunk into shadow at the edge of rising and falling, collecting the daily life that cannot be disposed of by ordinary people and the leftover items and residues that failed to catch on the speedy train of modernization.

The spaces in the city praised as the "Celestial Dragon Kingdom" emit the smell of the past and the odor that has just arrived. The "Earthly Dragon Kingdom" is like a parallel universe, a tenebrous existence in the city. Inglorious city landscape. Shameful locality. However, they have nourished artists' and writers' inspiration, which then presented in the form of eerie ghost stories. Half genuine, half fictional, these stories perforate the city and create a multidimensional world.

2.
We can discover the city's unique melancholy from the artists' marginal urban landscapes and put together a locality related to historical experience. These domestic artists seemed to possess the superpower specific to the islanders of seeing the other world, willing to synchronizingly present these two worlds that are in juxtaposition but at the same time in opposition. Intangible and quantum-entanglement-like "Ghosts stories" in *Perforated City* feature the narrow pathway of the human housing, the shimmering deities in Hell and haunted houses, and marginal and penetrable coloniality field. Like the fanfare of the Suona, they display a theater that several heterotopias coexist. The narrow pathway of human housing is where people pass through and stop by, the field that body and space are closely related.

Walkup apartments built in the 1960s have become a memorial space without conclusion, which cannot be abandoned nor can it be advanced. With people's certainty of their existence, hallucinations and illusions that roam in reality are what is left. In Chen Po-I's *Yin Yang Huajiang—Wandering Scenes of the Collective Housing*, he utilizes light and shadow photography techniques to dialogue with architect Chen Chi-Kwan's painting *Yin Yang*. With no residents in its scene, this work presents the publicness and privateness of Huajiang House in the 70s. Yu-Hao Hung uses 3D scanning in his *Wanderland* to record storefront overhangs in Wanhua, Taipei city's historical zone, and the ordinary people's daily life that developed underneath. These commercial and residential mixed-use storefront overhangs have mostly become the living place of hawkers, vendors, homeless people, passersby, residents, one that is similar to a home but not quite, or like a lively time capsule.

From the olden days to the future, did species evolve by natural selection or technological advancement? Can better species promise a better future in the search for the outer world? Between evolution and degeneration, the moon landing era's living space refers to the rapid acceleration of technological advances, like the front paws of a gigantic monster, hooking and clinging to the chest of the past. The central gallery stands the *Section Assembly Island* by Eric Chen, a layered wooden architectural theater that takes the walkup apartment as its prototype. Like a lively dovecote, it carries the connection between the building and the interpersonal relationship, and it also reveals the limited horizon in its interior. There are memory archives on this wooden isle that have lost temporality and permeated with the future vision from remote times.

On the scaffolding side of *Section Assembly Island* is Chu ChunTeng's *August 15th*. This spiral space belongs to the state of time stagnation, loss, and exploration, which walked by those with dislocated memory and cognition. At one end of the scaffolding is KUO I-Chen's sci-fi work that imagines the lunar landing era, *That's One Small Step for Mankind, One Giant Leap for Species*. With a non-front-end technology installation, it proposes a vision across time and space to reach the future. In another corner, Kuo Yu-Ping's *There Is a Light That Enters Houses With No Other House In Sight* uses multiple videos, sounds, and objects to create a spatial installation that seems to be under renovation and an abandoned space at the same time. The three films attempt to tell the Cold War era's desire when constructions were continuously carried out through modernization and the broken, reorganized destruction and construction. WU Yi-Hua's *Inside-out D-scène* dismembered and dislocated familiar daily objects and scenes poetically and mechanically.[6] Through the deployment of image illusions and dislocating heterogeneous objects, this scene suggests the surfeit of synthetic image in the era of artificial intelligence has led people into an Anthropocene utopia composed of disorder and restraint.

In addition to the community, individual residences are also the birthplace of vision. Art is mostly produced in Bohemian living environments. Teng Wen Hsin's *Murmur and Whisper* represents the artist's studio at Jingmei Xianjiyan, Taipei, founded in 2016, and the studio at a quiet alley near MOCA Taipei where she moved to two years later. Just as bacteria live on hosts, Teng established countless networks of symbiotic relations in the city's corner through a wide range of art and creative events. *Stargazing: 2014-2020* by Yi-Che, Chen was created during the artist's stay at the vacant space of Tamsui Old Street. To revive this deserted space's function, the artist cooperated with different communities, generating and expanding an interpersonal network in the art scene. These two works both involve in the future interpersonal space extended from the physical space in the past.

3.

Days subside, nights fall. In the mundane, polytheistic world, the shimmering deities in the haunted house are the alternative witnesses in the presence. Liang Ting-Yu's video installation *The Capturing River* displays the border area among Taoyuan's Daxi, Longtan, Fuxing, and Hsinchu's Guanxi, which was the locale of historical conflicts between the indigenous community and the Han people.[7] From the interweaving narratives told by elders in indigenous and Hakka communities, the death location of past conflicts, tribal memories, folklore and legends, supernatural experience form a site where the communities' distant memory and the pantheistic cosmos overlap. Based on the artist's fictional text, Yan Chung-Hsien's *Hell* visualizes the trip to Hell in Taiwanese folklore, building out the vision of the judge king's palace in Han people's belief with soft materials. ZHANG XU zhan's *Si So Mi* recreates a festive carnival of the dead with the marching band songs played the funerary procession and paper-made rat figures.

In Southeast Asia's contemporary cultural exchanges, the indigenous community's and the Han people's supernatural spaces and the heterotopias and fictional spaces where ghosts in the countryside and urban legends intertwined are intangible cultural legacy shared internationally. LIN, Yi-Chi's *Running Stitch— Bangkok* is a work created during an artist residency in Thailand. LIN conducted random, guerilla-style interviews on Bangkok's streets and brought together supernatural experiences gathered from three areas in the city. The interviews begin with this line: "I have met no spirits here, but I have my story to tell." The monumental deities' statues scattered around the island once again testify Taiwan's living space has a geographical characteristic of humans' coexistence, deities, and ghosts. YAO Jui Chung's *Incarnation* is a photography series featuring the colossal deities' statues in Taiwan, which informs the relations of folk life, religion, and politico-economic in Taiwan's geographic space. To create this work of social spectacle, YAO combines three-channel video with a mixture of NASA's recording of cosmic sounds and religious festivals – an uncanny yet magical sound that resonates in the room.

4.

Marginal and serving fields also link the connection of the "instrumentalized" body and space. With HSU, HUI-CHING's experience as a flight attendant, *Border Roaming* presents how flight attendants convert into different serving identity in aircraft cabins. In the video, the female flight attendant provides objects on customers' requests and actively and passively changes her outfit to reveal a multi-perspective body landscape. "Food delivery," the emerging consumption modes in recent years, is the inspiration for Huang Yen-Chao's *Food Winger*. The artist regards the food deliverers' daily routes, the circling intervention of streets and alleys every day, as a new form of a human geographical map and a metaphor for the instrumentalization of life.

As coloniality crept in, the landscape of the commercial world has gradually changed. Tang Tang-Fa's *Indonesian Grocery Store in Taiwan* displays objects that connect the Indonesians in Taiwan with their homeland, showcasing the material world and commercial culture of recent Southeast Asian immigrants. The intervention of foreign objects discloses the inevitable change in Taiwan's street views. The landscape called "local locality" will assemble the "locality" of the past and the "new locality" in perforation. They are no longer ruins or residues but odors and additives that are half familiar, half strange.

Every perforation story of each city has its locality. Although the population, economic, and cultural infiltration of new immigrants' lifestyle and custom do not necessarily change the city's spaces, they still occur as a fluid phenomenon of "locality vs. coloniality," remaining a ruined and pervasive state. The thriving "Celestial Dragon Kingdom" could be in expansion, but it could also be withering. The phenomena of perforation can be witnessed in both buildings and the interrelationship in communities. The word "ruin" can be an erosive verb or a noun that forms an entity; it constructs a city's body landscape and provides a warning vision like the "Five Decays of the Deva." [8]

All cities in the perforation process among the global urban competition possess their "ruin stories" and the contradictory "coloniality" brought by migration and technology. "Perforated City" as a metaphor of cities in modernizing Taiwan, the word "perforated" seems to be viewed as a symbol of penetration and ruin. Artists telling stories are under the sun or in the dark; some were already there, and others were summoned to the places. These works that are wandering in modernity are like verses of shadow created by the "presence" and "absence" of the artists, showcasing a visible but also invisible "Lost Earthly Dragon Kingdom."

Thus have I thought. If *Le Spleen de Paris* endeavors to mobilize the ghosts of a city with the eyes of a lonely city flaneur and his words, then this "Le Spleen de Tuã-ka-lak-pó" attempts to gather different visual landscape to summon the ghosts of a city and the social landscape where humans, deities, and ghosts coexist. This space is the reality and a spectacle, and with all its connections, it produces a vitality that cannot be replicated.

[1] Tuā-ka-lak is said to be originated from Ketagalan, one of the tribes of Pepohoan. A similar word Tagal means "swamp." Tuā-ka-lak was initially referring to the plain along the Xindian River banks in the Wanhua district of Old Taipei City. At the beginning of the 18th century, the Han people colonized Tuā-ka-lak and gradually expanded its realm. It was thus renamed as Tuā-ka-lak-pó. During the reign of the Qing dynasty Tongzhi Emperor, Tuā-ka-lak-pó covered the old town of today's Taipei City and New Taipei City. In 1902 the Japanese authority abolished Tuā-ka-lak-pó, the name of Tuā-ka-lak has faded into oblivion. This essay takes the idea of Le Spleen de Tuā-ka-lak-pó as a metaphor of the modern urban space development in northern Taiwan, signifying a living space in disguise with collective memories and amnesia that exist before and after the establishment of "Celestial Dragon Kingdom."

[2] Johann Jessen's article was published in 2006. This footnote refers to *Perforated City: Leipzig's Model of Urban Shrinkage Management* by Daniel Florentin, published in Berkeley Planning Journal (Volume 23, 2010). Online source: https://escholarship.org/uc/item/97p1p1jx (2020/07/05)

[3] Leipzig, Germany has been continuously shrinking since 1966. It was not until 1989 did the socialist transition transform this phenomenon. Unlike other East German cities, such as Dresden, Leipzig decided to adapt to shrinkage and perforation at an early stage to manage the shrinkage process and take advantage of the change to maintain the city's image.

[4] According to Daniel Florentin's study, there were three main axes in Leipzig's planning strategy: preserving the architectural heritage, considered a trademark of the city, creating green spaces and open spaces to replace dilapidated housing estates, and supporting the creation of a micro-scale hierarchy of centres. It was not surprising that Leipzig witnessed planning territorial competition and polarisation in the course of urban planning.

[5] "Celestial Dragons" is a Taiwanese internet slang taken from the nobles' name in the Japanese manga series One Piece. It is now used to describe those who sojourn or reside in Taipei, disconnected from reality and unaware of the mass's sufferings. The "Celestial Dragon Kingdom" has become the most modern nickname for Taipei City, and according to real estate prices and the types of building, there are different economic classes, such as "Celestial Dragon District" and "Celestial Dragon Town."

[6] Wu mentions in his statement that he drew inspiration from German playwright Heiner Müller's *Die Hamletmachine*. Please refer to MOCA Taipei's exhibition information.

[7] Please refer to the documents at the exhibition.

[8] "Five Decays of the Deva" is a Buddhist expression describing the phenomena that occur when the deva in heaven is at death's door. "The Five Decays" includes "Major Five Decays" and "Minor Five Decays.' With Major Five Decays, devas will fall into the cycle of death and rebirth; with Minor Five Decays, devas with virtuous roots and practice the disciple of Buddhism would have a chance to regain vitality.

在流動的縫隙之間——
行走「穿孔城市」的策展閱讀

文｜張晴文

●穿孔 1：母土

城市是黃海鳴長年觀察、落實寫作、策展、街區行動的場域。多年以來，他除了致力當代藝術的觀察和研究，也投入許多藝術生態研究和改造行動的策畫，以及具有社區總體營造功能的戶外裝置展覽策畫。2000 年左右，他曾在〈網路時代的城市美學——以「整個城市」為審美對象的基本格局〉一文中，描述自己於中年突然意識到「整個城市」對他所造成的震撼，並且發出許多提問：

> 難道不能夠把「整個城市」當作一件「大作品」來看？或當作一個審美的對象？一般我們總是把輪廓模糊的「整個城市」當作其它的局部事物以及較小型的「造形藝術作品」的「背景」，難道它不也是一件「大作品」？一件由許多人共同集體創作出來的「大作品」。[......] 也許是因為我們距離城市太近，永遠只能看到一小部分，所以無從把城市當作一件輪廓清楚的「大作品」。或是說，如果硬要把它當作一件「大作品」來看時，必須是透過非常複雜和大量的記憶片段的合成，才能夠同時在我們的心眼前呈現，因此很難用一件「大作品」的觀念來面對它。難道我們一直只能用「模糊的背景」來稱呼它？只是因為我們沒有鉅細靡遺的觀察，結構性的認識和高度的統合成象的能力，就一直把它當作背景來看？[1]

這一段寫於 20 年前對於觀看城市的反思，提點了我們在 2020 年進入「穿孔城市」展場之時能夠著眼的視角。

這些年來，黃海鳴在城市之中穿梭行走，以相機鉅細靡遺地捕捉各個觸動心緒的景觀、各種震撼及發現，並且累積成對於城市的認識和思維。雖說城市可以成為我們觀看的對象，但有趣的是我們的觀察也在城市之內發生。我們在城市裡生活、移動、體驗，並且形塑了它的樣子。在「穿孔城市」的廊道及展間移動時，我們確實看見了一個城市「不只做為某種模糊背景」的樣態，它展現了自身（儘管展覽並未明確以某一個城市為範本），也呈現了臺灣城市化過程的諸種面向，亦即，顯現了當年黃海鳴在文中提及的「積澱的城市聚落」之面貌。它是全民集體創作的結果，也是臺灣「不斷轉變的大地之母」——「這塊母土，坐落在吸取了所有垃圾及養分，由民眾集體地構築起來『積澱的城市聚落』的內部」[2]：

> 這本身就是流動的「集體的、原始的城市肉體」，這團流動的「城市肉體」，不只是在百貨公司展示櫃前的所有通道及廣場，更是在這些表層和表層後面的所有管道、隔間、儲藏、服務、休息的空間，以及大街小巷的生活空間之內，他們就是城市大身體的骨骼、肌肉、內臟。[3]

如果這塊「城市肉體」仍在不斷成長（同時衰老）、增生（同時崩毀），2020 年的「穿孔城市」則是策展人所提出的，數十年來沉浸於城市的觀察與思考的報告，同時也是其近年少見地以館舍空間為基地，所呈現的策展。

●穿孔 2：對照

在策展論述中，黃海鳴提及「穿孔城市」的幾層意涵，簡而言之可以歸納為四個面向：(1) 城市聚落中人際關係的疏離化，以及街區邊緣化沒落之後其間活性網絡的失效；(2) 將公寓做為一個隱喻，透過打開障壁的過程，使原本不可見的各種關係現形；(3) 貫穿在整個城市之中，無可抵擋的各種力量運作；以及 (4) 穿越層層隔離，互助連結網的形構，具有生產力的一面。在這四個面向「穿孔」的演繹方法上，策展人將藝術家分為七個不同的思維組別，並將作品配置於展場內外。

當觀眾走近台北當代藝術館，首先即能在入口廣場看見一座螺旋窄梯，直上平常觀眾無法進入的大廳露台。這一座帶有些許工業風的簡潔梯子，同時以鑽孔以及搭建的意象，來打通某些區域。這是展覽由外觀之的第一個視覺印象，來自郭奕臣《這是人類的一小步，物種的一大步》作品的一部分。然而走進展場之後，迎面而來是一隻吊掛的巨大老鼠殘骸。這件鄧堯鴻的《繭影》以誇張的比例暗示著觀者：我們即將和城市中竄逃的老鼠相互易位。我們的身體相對縮小至能夠穿梭在城市縫隙中的尺寸，以便走入這一座穿孔的城市。這身在鏡廳之中不斷返照自身的鼠屍與殘骸，將觀看的人也納入其中。我們都被困在這一沒有出口與入口的無限迷宮之中。就這樣，透過卡夫卡式的荒謬魔法，點石成金地使觀眾能夠穿透所有可見與不可見的屏蔽，微觀都市的殘餘與生活屑末所搭建的花園，以及種種在城市間流動的意識與景觀。這是展覽給觀眾的第二個視覺印象。以上兩個立即的視覺感，也為整個展覽確立了一種靈活且必要的視角。要探查城市裡幽微的各種穿孔的力量與現象，走入這一塊經過時間發酵、經由人和各種生物的身體穿越所產生的別具味道的乳酪，需要某些容許虛構的眼光。當觀眾走在展場之中，館舍內外與各個樓層之間的意象穿透、廊道與樓梯的通連、敞開與幽閉的展場之間，有著層層疊疊的呼應關係，無不回應著展覽的主題。這是策展人在展場佈局上的心思，也使得這項展覽能夠在一個巨大的主題之下，透過視覺的觸動，支撐起各種龐雜且具有張力的開展與變化，使觀眾得以透過展覽，深入這一座位於城市之內的另一座隱喻城市，並看見自己置身其中。進入展場之前，位於 105 對面的廊道，展示著策展人多年來穿梭城市之間所捕捉的聚落型態。這一帶著歷史縱深、地理廣度的照片牆，以及各種具有極大穿透能力的網路社群符號，交織成這項展覽的另類地圖。這些照片裡的角落似曾相識，某些建設巨大而恢弘，有些角落隱蔽卻醇厚，它們容納各式身體在其間生活，它們的起落也說明了城市文化的變貌。這一面牆在展覽中和作品有著內在的對應關係，更是策展人在論述與作品結構之外重要的概念闡述，更立體化地展現了「穿孔城市」在現實中的對照，是一則屬於我們的故事。

●穿孔 3：連接

透過策展人提出解讀「穿孔城市」的四個提示，我們閱讀到作品在此一主題脈絡之中所坐落的議題位置。對於這些議題，策展人不以區域的劃分方式闡述，而是讓這些相互牽連的議題散置在展場之內。導引觀者的，不是「穿孔城市」的論述地圖，而是每件作品各自的意象，及其與環境、前後作品產生的閱讀脈絡，以至於它們經常在展場中呈現二到三件作品相鄰對話的密切關係，例如姚瑞中《巨神連線》與顏忠賢《地獄變相》；陳伯義《步移景換·華江陰陽》與洪譽豪《無以為家》；梁廷毓《襲奪之河》與林弈綺《運行針：曼谷》；吳宜樺《裡外急轉彎的 D 場景》與郭俞平《一盞燈進入房子，看不到其他房子》；鄧雯馨《牆角窸窣囈語》與陳毅哲《觀星者：2014-2020》；以及陳宣誠《剖視島》、郭奕臣《這是人類的一小步，物種的一大步》、朱駿騰《八月十五》等。

就展覽的動線而言，台北當代藝術館充滿歷史感的紅磚建築體、它所帶有的政治與文化脈絡，提供了「穿孔城市」另一個現實的參照。美術館內部展場以區隔的房間為基本型態，這些牆面似也回應著策展論述中不斷提及的居住空間的封閉與隔離現實。走進左側展場，首先是以巨大三連屏呈現不斷流轉切換的民間巨大佛像攝影，《巨神連線》所展示的是穿透世間慾念的顯影，而鄰近的《地獄變相》則一反莊嚴的敘事，以戲謔的嘲諷故作姿態地展現不怕死與怕死的人間矛盾。洪譽豪的作品以 3D 掃描的技術及現場裝置，重現破落區域裡的幽暗面，而展間之外與之相對的陳伯義作品，則以拼接的攝影畫面無言敘說了街道之外，民居之間相互串連如同迷宮自成一格的小聚落，這一類型的住宅在臺灣有其發展的歷史背景，而今逐漸轉化為城市中各種意義上的廢墟。

展場中，也有幾件作品扮演重要的展場空間鏈結者，包括通連館內外的郭奕臣作品、鄧堯鴻的《繭影》穿透一樓與二樓的視野、唐唐發＋FIDATI(PINDY WINDY) 在樓梯間擘劃出跨文化對話的轉折空間、黃彥超《Food Winger》以不斷滑行的食物快遞者和振翅的蜂鳥在煽動焦慮之餘暗示了流竄城市的疾行步調、由張徐展《Si So Mi》延伸的乾癟動物與鏡子陰魂不散地出現在全館空間，這些在牆角惱人的死亡意象卻以荒謬喜感的姿態現身，同時也以懸殊的比例展現了與鄧堯鴻《繭影》之間的對應關係。從展場的起點與終點，我們透過（化身為）老鼠或者失去肉體的魂魄，把城市裡各種孔隙閱覽了一遍。

在二樓展場中，201 展間內的幾件作品有著密切的連結關係。如果說二樓廊道起始點上《Food Winger》在城市的飛速穿梭，是整個展覽裡極富「穿孔城市」動能意象的表徵，那麼朱駿騰《八月十五》中，那些不曾停下卻不知目的的腳步、定睛觀看彷彿時光凍結的凝視，以及從監視器路過卻不知去向的疑問，則成為另類的對照。當滿溢的水杯碎裂，「穿孔城市」中的迷途並不會停止。轉角下樓，牆角有延伸自張徐展作品的一句「留下來，或我跟妳走」，成為展覽最終耐人尋味的一則邀請或提問。

●穿孔 4：穿孔

「穿孔城市」是展策展人多年來關切城市樣貌及內在的成果。本展中，透過作品內部敘事的相互折射，為這項展覽的命題指出許多發現與創造的面貌。關於閱讀城市紋理，黃海鳴亦曾在 2007 年的一項書寫中提及其重要性：

> 我們應該滿足於只是將這些片段拼貼成超現實主義的城市文本的閱讀行動，而不是努力想把城市中疏離的人、差異的城市文本拉在一起交流、對話、共同創造不知道什麼東西的另一種藝術意志。[4]

對比於某種投入創造的願想，描繪並指認城市的變貌，其實正是認識自身的不二途徑。回到前文曾經提到的「積澱的城市聚落」做為我們生長與活動的所在，每一座城市將會在時空的綿延之下，不斷地以各種方式和其間的生命交織為無可分割的巨大結構。而我們終將與這塊乳酪合而為一，成為彼此牽掛的一部分。

[1] 黃海鳴，〈網路時代的城市美學──以「整個城市」為審美對象的基本格局〉，收入李既鳴總編，《從「身體」到「城市」的閱讀》。臺北市：臺北市立美術館，2000，頁 174-175。

[2] 同前註，頁 178-179。

[3] 同前註，頁 179。

[4] 黃海鳴，〈城市地面天空大樓間的影像／櫥窗／劇場─影像／櫥窗／劇場效應與疏離城市中可能的交互關係網絡〉，收入李既鳴總編，《影像研究・藝術思維》。臺北市：臺北市立美術館，2007，頁 257。

Between the Changing Crevasses: Curatorial Readings on *Perforated City*

Text | Chang Ching-Wen

● Perforation 1: Motherland

The urban setting has long been the backdrop of Huang Hai-Ming's observations, writings, curation, and street block events. For many years, Huang has not only been dedicated to observations and research on contemporary art but also the research of the ecology of art and the organization of renovation events, as well as outdoor installations that encourage community revitalization. Around the year 2000, Huang described the shock the idea of "the city as a whole" brought forth during his middle-age years and proposed several questions in the article "Urban Aesthetics in the Internet Age: The Fundamental Structure of the Aesthetic Viewing of 'the City as a Whole':"

Can't we view "the city as a whole" as a "large-scale work?" Or an object of aesthetic appreciation? We tend to view "the city as a whole" as the blurry backdrop of partial incidents or smaller works of "plastic arts." But isn't the city a "large-scale work" in itself? One created collectively by the people [......] Perhaps we will always be limited to partial views because we are too close to the city and therefore can never be able to see the city as a "large-scale work" with distinct borders and outlines. In other words, if we insist on viewing the city as a "large-scale work," we must put together large quantities of memory segments that are immensely complex to be able to piece together the image in our minds; hence the difficulty of viewing the city as a "large-scale work." But can we merely refer to it as a "blurry backdrop?" Perhaps it is because we have not observed in great detail, through structural understanding, and with high integration skills, and can therefore merely view it as a background?[1]

This passage of observations towards the city written 20 years ago reminds us of the perspective we might adopt when entering the exhibition space of *Perforated City* in 2020.

Throughout recent years, Huang has strolled the city with a camera in hand, capturing in detail the heart-touching, awe-inducing sceneries or observations in the city, which accumulate into understandings and musings towards the urban environment. Although cities may become viewing objects, interestingly, the city is also the setting where our observations occur. We live, move, and gain experiences within the city, and in turn, shape the urban landscape. When moving around in the corridors and exhibition spaces of *Perforated City*, we see a city that is "more than a blurry backdrop," but a manifestation of itself (although the exhibition does not identify any specific city) while presenting the various aspects of the urbanization of Taiwan, namely the imagery of the "accumulation of urban settlement" mentioned by Huang in his article. What Huang describes is the result of collective creativity and Taiwan as "the everchanging motherland"—"This motherland exists amid the 'accumulation of urban settlement,' which absorbs all waste and nutrients and is constructed collectively by its people[2]:"

> This is essentially a changing "collective, primitive flesh of the city." This lump of changing "flesh of the city" not only appears in the aisles and squares in front of department store display windows but also in all conduits, compartments, service spaces, resting places within and behind the surface layers, as well as the living spaces in streets and alleys; they are the bones, muscles, and organs of the body of the city. [3]

If this "flesh of the city" continues to grow (and age) and proliferate (and collapse), 2020's *Perforated City* is the curator's report on decades of observations and contemplations of the city, as well as one of the few site-specific exhibitions in recent years.

● Perforation 2: Comparison

In his curatorial statement, Huang Hai-Ming mentions the different layers of meanings of *Perforated City*. Simply put, the concept involves four aspects: (1) The alienation of interpersonal relationships in cities and active networks becoming useless after street blocks decline and become marginalized; (2) The apartment becomes a metaphor that exposes barriers that were previously invisible; (3)

The operation of irresistible forces that fill the entire city; and (4) the aspect of productivity by penetrating barriers and forming networks. Based on the four interpretations of "perforation," the curator separates the artists into seven different themes and places the works both inside and outside exhibition spaces.

As viewers approach the Museum of Contemporary Art (MOCA) Taipei, they are first greeted by a narrow winding staircase that leads to the terrace, which is usually inaccessible to visitors. This minimalistic, industrial-style ladder conveys the imagery of perforation and construction, connecting separated areas. Here, viewers receive their first impression of the exhibition, and the staircase is a part of Kuo I-Chen's *That's One Small Step for Mankind, One Giant Leap for Species*. However, the viewer is greeted by a large suspended rat carcass upon entering the exhibition space: Deng Yau-Horng's Shadow of a Cocoon. Deng's work uses exaggerated proportions to hint to the viewer: We are about to switch places with the scattering city rats. Relatively speaking, our body shrinks to a size allowing us to move through crevasses and enter this perforated city. The image of the rat carcass and remains placed in a mirrored room is constantly being reflected, with the viewer situated within the same space. We are all trapped in this endless maze without an entrance or exit. This Kafkaesque magic enlightens the audience to penetrate all visible and invisible barriers, enabling microcosmic observations towards the garden built with the fragments of the city and remnants of life, as well as the various thoughts and sceneries that flow throughout the city; this is the second visual impression of the exhibition. The two instantaneous visuals provide an agile and necessary perspective for the exhibition. To examine the nuanced forces and phenomena of perforations, and to enter this cheese that has been fermented with time and diffuses the unique aroma created by the bodies of different people and organisms, viewers must allow space for fabrication.

As viewers move around the venue, they will find that the penetrating imageries inside and outside the building and the different floors, the corridor and staircase pathways, and the open and enclosed exhibition spaces, all connect to the exhibition theme and echo one another on different aspects. Through visual sensations, the thoughtful design of the curator allows the exhibition to include the different and complex developments and changes under the large topic. The curation allows viewers to explore deeply into the metaphorical city-within-the-city while seeing themselves within the setting. Before entering the exhibition, viewers will see that images of different urban scenarios that the curator has captured across cities throughout the years are displayed in the hallway opposite 105. This photography wall that harbors historical depth and geographical width and the piercing symbols used in internet social media weave into an alternative map of the exhibition. The corners captured in the images seem familiar: some architectures are grand and vast, while some are mellow but invisible, each sheltering different bodies and lives while their rise and fall are manifestations of the changes of the city. There is an internal correspondence between the photography wall and the works of the exhibition, and the wall is a significant concept that is independent of the curator's statement and the structure of the works, giving a more dynamic reference of Perforated City in reality and presenting a story of our own.

● Perforation 3: Connection

Following the four clues from the curator, we are able to interpret the works within the context of the theme *Perforated City*. Instead of creating separate areas for different themes, the curator allows related topics to be scattered across the display space. Viewers are not guided by a map of the exhibition discourse; instead, each work has its own imagery and context with its surroundings and nearby works. As a result, works that are placed within close proximity often convey intertwined messages in groups of two or three. For instance, Yao Jui Chung's *Incarnation* and Yan Chung-Hsien's *Hell*; Chen Po-I's *Yin Yang Huajiang— Wandering Scenes of the Collective Housing* and Yu-Hao Hung's *Wanderland*, Liang Ting-Yu's *The Capturing River* and Lin Yi-Chi's *Running Stitch – Bangkok*, Wu Yi-Hua's *Inside-out D-scène* and Kuo Yu-Ping's *There Is a Light That Enters Houses With No Other House In Sight*, Teng Wen Hsin's *Murmur and Whisper* and Chen Yi-Che's *Stargazing: 2014-2020*, Eric Chen's *Section Assembly Island* and Kuo I-Chen's *That's One Small Step for Mankind, One Giant Leap for Species* and Chu ChunTeng's *August 15th*.

In terms of traffic flow, MOCA Taipei's historic red-brick architecture and its inherent political and cultural context becomes another example for *Perforated City*. The exhibition spaces of the museum are based on the separated rooms of the building, and the walls seem like a response to the enclosed living spaces and isolation mentioned in the curatorial statement. As viewers enter the exhibition space on the left, they are greeted by a large three-channel video installation screening images of huge Buddha statues. Incarnation is a work that showcases images that penetrate worldly yearnings, while its nearby work *Hell* abandons solemn narratives and instead explores the human contradiction between fearlessness and fearfulness towards death through ridicule and sarcasm. Yu-Hao Hung's *Wanderland* re-presents the murky scenes of abandoned areas through 3D scanning and on-site installations, while Chen Po-I's work, which echoes the theme but is placed in another exhibition room, expresses how residents group into small maze-like settlements that exist outside of streets through collaged photography images. The developments of these living arrangements have their historical context but the scenes are now becoming wastelands in various urban settings.

A few of the works serve as significant connecting pieces throughout the exhibition. Kuo I-Chen's work connects the interior and exterior spaces of the venue, Deng Yau-Horng's *Shadow of a Cocoon* permeates the views of the first and second floor, Tang Tang-Fa and FIDATI(PINDY WINDY) carve out a transition space for cross-cultural dialogue on the staircase, Huang Yen-Chao's *Food Winger* hints to the fast tempo and rousing anxiety of a fast-paced city through the image of a skateboarding food deliverer and a hummingbird flapping its wings, and the shriveled animals and mirrors from ZHANG XU zhan's *Si So Mi* appear all over the venue, forming ludicrous comedy with its imagery of death while corresponding to Deng Yau-Horng's *Shadow of a Cocoon* through disparate proportions. From start to finish of the exhibition, we are taken through a reading of the perforations of the city through the perspective (or by becoming) a rat or a bodiless spirit.

The works within exhibition room 201 on the second floor are tightly-knitted together. If the fast-moving images of *Food Winger* at the start of the second-floor corridor serves as the rich dynamic imagery of *Perforated City*, then the moving but desultory paces, time-stopping gazes, and questions provoked by security camera images of people passing by in Chu ChunTeng's *August 15th* become an alternative analogy. The wanderings of *Perforated City* do not stop when the water cup overflows and cracks. Turn a corner and head downstairs; the sentence "stay, or let me come with you," which extends from ZHANG XU zhan's work, becomes an intriguing final invitation or proposition of the exhibition.

● Perforation 4: Perforation

Perforated City is the fruit of the curator's many years of keen observation of the outer and inner states of the city. Through the mutual refractions of the internal narrative of the works, this exhibition presents many discovered and created aspects of the topic. As for the reading of the city's textures, Huang Hai-Ming wrote about its importance in an article in 2007:

> We should be content about interpretations based on piecing segments into a surreal urban text and not strive to bring isolated individuals and different urban texts together for interaction, dialogue, or to create some unknown artistic resolve.[4]

Compared with aspirations to participate in the creative process, to describe and identify the appearance of the city is, in fact, the only path towards self-understanding. As previously mentioned, with the "accumulation of urban settlement" as the setting of our growth and activities, each city continues to weave and expand throughout time and space with different methods and the lives within. We will merge as one with this piece of cheese, each inseparable from the other.

[1] Hai-Ming Huang, "Urban Aesthetics in the Internet Age: The Fundamental Structure of the Aesthetic Viewing of 'the City as a Whole' ," included in *From Body to City: A Reading*, chief editor Li Chi-Ming. Taipei City: Taipei Fine Arts Museum, 2000, pp. 174-175.

[2] ibid., pp. 178-179.

[3] ibid., p. 179.

[4] Hai-Ming Huang, "Images/Windows/Theatre-Images/Windows/Theater Effects within the Land, Sky, and Buildings in Cities and a Possible Interactive Network for the City of Alienation," included in *Studied Images, Artistic Thought*, chief editor Chi-Ming Li. Taipei City: Taipei Fine Arts Museum, 2007, p. 257.

Artists

藝術家

Fixation, Split and
Entanglement of
Social Relations and Networks

第
01
組

社會網絡關係的固著
／脫落
／糾結牽制

● Chen Po-I
陳伯義

Yin Yang Huajiang— Wandering Scenes of the Collective Housing
《步移景換・華江陰陽》

數位輸出 C-Print ｜ 757 x 75 cm ｜ 2020

華江整宅建於 70 年代，是當時極具現代感的建築規劃。一、二樓原為商業使用，後因萬華榮景不再，二樓騎樓就漸漸變成居民住宅的空間延伸，從公共空間轉為私有的社區空間。特殊的廊道系統將四棟建築物連成一氣，建構了建築的群聚特性，然而連結至街道的樓梯，又讓社區生活具備了特殊的開放性。其中，一樓至二樓的樓梯設計，寬度較一般住宅樓梯寬出許多；至三樓空中花園的樓梯則變成十分狹窄。換言之，樓梯的寬度也創造出空間公共性與私密性間的差異。這樣環形廊道與樓梯的設計，讓建築的平面與垂直空間都兼具了特殊的穿透性與流動性。

陳伯義以華江整宅六名建築師之一的陳其寬所繪畫作《陰陽》所啟發，以類似卷軸的長幅方式呈現，利用攝影的光影轉換，表現出空間的虛實變化，移步換景、視點游移，顯露出具時間性的日常片段，觀者隨著攝影師的視線與身體漫遊，移轉穿透於建築與城市之間的交互關係，以及公共與私有空間的內外模糊曖昧狀態。

Huajiang House was built in the 70s, and was one of the most modern architectural projects at the time. The first and second floors were originally designed for commercial purposes. However, after Wanhua District fell from its grace, the second-floor open corridors used by the residents have gradually become the extension of the residential units in the buildings, turning public space into private communal space. The unique design of the open corridor system connects the four buildings, architecturally creating a communal quality; nonetheless, the stairways leading to the streets on the ground floor add a distinctive sense of openness to the communal living. It is worth mentioning that the stairways from the first floor to the second floor are much wider than stairways in common residential buildings, whereas those connecting the second floor to the third-floor garden are noticeably narrower. In other words, the width of stairways also varies as a means to differentiate public and private spaces. The circular corridor system and the design of stairways form the characteristic perviousness and flow both in terms of the horizontal and vertical planes of the architecture.

Chen Po-I draws his inspiration from the *Yin Yang* series painted by Chen Chi-Kwan, one of the six architects of Huajiang House, and uses a long horizontal scroll for this work. With photographic variations informed by light and shadow, the artist delineates the real and virtual changes in the space, depicting wandering scenes with moving perspectives to highlight the daily fragments characterized by time. The audience therefore wanders through the photographer's eyes and movement, and traverses the interrelations between the architecture and the city as well as the ambiguous state that blurs the boundary between public and private spaces.

● Yu-Hao Hung
洪譽豪

Wanderland
《無以為家》

三頻道錄像 Three-Channel Video ｜ 5 min. ｜ 2020

臺灣的騎樓空間為因應臺灣炎熱多雨的天氣而發展出來，經由清代政策的推廣與日治時代的法令規定後，成為了臺灣特有的建築景觀，不僅提供行人遮風蔽雨的行走空間，也是店舖空間的延伸，形成公領域與私領域交雜共處的特殊樣態。

《無以為家》主要取材自萬華的騎樓空間。在這個經歷過繁華與衰敗的臺北舊城區，騎樓是一個留有時間軌跡的通道，也是交織著攤販、過客、住民、遊民、茶室、小吃攤的生活場域，乘載了長年佇留於此的人們之記憶與情感，似家，又非家。作品以 3D 掃描紀錄騎樓內的常民生活，然而此種凝鍊卻並非靜止的，取得的點雲 (Point cloud) 數據彷彿是逐漸堆積的時間晶體，在動態的流動中不斷地聚合，又再次離散，人們生活的軌跡進入了時間之流中，讓每個瞬間都不斷連續與綿延。

Historically speaking, storefront overhangs in Taiwan were created due to the island's warm and rainy climate. After the related policies implemented during the Qing regime and the regulations in the period of Japanese rule, storefront overhangs have become a characteristic architectural sight in Taiwan, not only providing pedestrians a sheltering space from wind and rain but also serving as an extension of stores— they are, in short, a unique interface between the public and private spaces.

Wanderland is based on the storefront overhangs in Wanhua District. In this historical zone of Taipei that has witnessed as much glory of the city as its decline, the storefront overhangs form a corridor that has preserved traces of time and a common site where vendors, passersby, residents, homeless people, tea parlors and street delis intermix, carrying memories and feelings of people who have spent years living and lingering in this space, one that is like home but not quite. The work uses 3D scanning to record people's daily life in the storefront overhangs that seems coagulated yet constant moving. The gathered point cloud data resemble gradually accumulated crystallization of time, and in the dynamic flow of time, it has continuously converged and dispersed again. When the trajectory of people's life merges with the river of time, every moment in their life has joined together and become an ever-extending continuation.

● Chu ChunTeng
朱駿騰

August 15th
《八月十五》

七頻道影像、十二軌聲音多媒體影音裝置

7-Channel Video, 12-Tracks Sounds Multimedia Installation │ 12:05 min. │ 2017

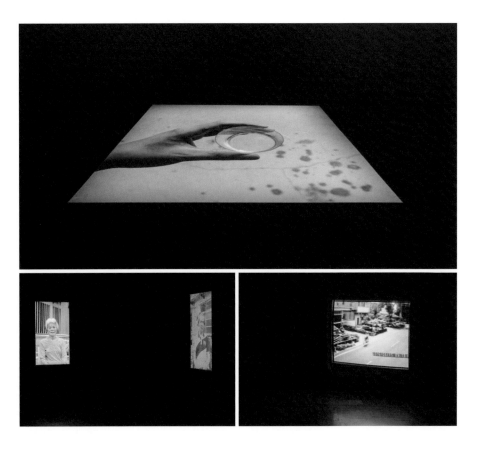

《八月十五》紀錄了因各種原因造成記憶與認知錯位的人，以看似平行零散的影像與聲音訴說著關於時間／失去／尋找的狀態。展場內的三幅動態肖像與觀者面對面凝視，但視覺的溝通連結卻已在某處斷裂，無法抵達被攝者心靈深處；監視器停格畫面標註著「2016 年 8 月 15 日」，記錄一名至今未能尋獲的失蹤老人身影；家屬尋找失蹤者的話語，若即若離地碎散在展場；水滴滴入杯中的聲響，有如失控的計時器般逐漸加速，最終盈滿並摔落碎裂。停滯的狀態與生存的內部時間，形成一個難以輕易言說的內外平行對照。

雙頻道投影則是拍攝療養院中一名罹患阿茲海默症的長者，在清醒與恍惚之間於院內空間反覆緩慢繞行與駐足；右方晃動、失焦、不穩定的倒退行走畫面，彷彿進入了患者的內部身體與存在狀態，院外庭園重重的柵欄和圍牆，也暗示著他人難以進入患者心靈迷宮的外邊狀態。

August 15th documents various individuals suffering from memory issues or cognitive dislocation with parallel yet scattered images and sounds that speak about the status of time/lost/searching. Three motion portraits are presented in the exhibition, seemingly gazing at the audience; however, the visual communication is already ruptured and the audience is unable to perceive the depth of the subjects' minds. The image of the surveillance camera, marked with the date of August 15th, 2016, shows an elder that remains unfound to date. Words uttered by his family members are scattered around the exhibition. The sound of water dripping into a glass gradually accelerates like a timer that is slowly losing control; eventually, the glass is filled up, falls to the ground and breaks into pieces. The still state and the internal time of the survived form an inexpressible contrast between the external and the inner worlds.

The two-channel projection shows an elderly patient with Alzheimer in a nursing home, who appears to be repeatedly pacing and standing still in the institution, seemingly in a state of being half-conscious. On the right, the shaky, out-of-focus, unsteady image of moving backwards, in a way, suggests the unstable inner world of the patient, reminding viewers of his physical condition and state of existence. The fences and walls surrounding the garden of the nursing home also hint at the fact that people are outsiders that cannot enter the internal labyrinth of the patient.

 **Eric Chen**
陳宣誠

Section Assembly Island
《剖視島》

空間裝置 Space Installation ｜ 尺寸因空間而異 Dimensions Variable ｜ 2020

「步登公寓」為 60-70 年代大量興建的四、五層樓無電梯集合住宅，為臺灣住居形式邁向現代化的重要建築樣態。垂直化的發展，改變了人們的居住形式，從個體到群體的集居行為，讓鄰里關係與城市環境有了巨大的改變。其中，樓梯成為意識他者與外在環境的交流空間；窗戶和陽台也讓私宅的日常景觀成為城市集體樣貌的構成要素；公寓的屋頂則提供了觀看城市的不同視角。

《剖視島》以「步登公寓」為原型，企圖以一種剖面的集合，形成不同視角觀看的立面，藉以想像城市發展中日常生活的流動，呈現多方向、持續生長、脆弱多孔、層疊與觸覺的場域特質。這件位於展場中央的作品，讓觀眾隨著路徑改變觀看的視角，視線穿越層層疊疊的窗戶與房間，直到屋頂俯瞰整個展場，藉以逐步想像建築／藝術作品內外空間的對應關係。同時，《剖視島》也緊密結合了藝術家郭奕臣與朱駿騰的作品，乘載了作品間相互穿透與連結的可能性。

"Walkup apartment" refers to those four- or five-story buildings extensively built for congregate housing during the 60s and 70s, which has been an important architectural form that marks Taiwan's modernization in housing. The vertical development changed the way of housing from individual residences to collective living, and introduced a great shift in the relationship between people, their neighbors and urban environment. In this architectural form, stairway serves as a space of exchange where one becomes aware of others and the external environment. Also, windows and balconies of individual apartments constitute the daily cityscape of collective life. The rooftops of these apartments, on the other hand, offer a different angle to observe the city.

Section Assembly Island draws inspiration from "walkup apartment" and reveals facades from different perspectives through the section assembly to imagine the flow of daily life in urban development, presenting the multi-directional, ever-growing, fragile, porous, layered and tactile qualities of such a site. This work, displayed at the center of the gallery room, allows evolving perspectives as audiences change their viewing route, letting their vision go through layers of windows and rooms before bringing them to the rooftop where the entire gallery room can be seen. By doing so, it gradually unveils an interrelated relationship between spaces within and without the architecture/artwork. Meanwhile, *Section Assembly Island* is closely linked with the works respectively created by KUO I-Chen and Chu ChunTeng, and adds another possibility of correlation and connection between these works.

● YAO Jui Chung
姚瑞中

Incarnation
《巨神連線》

三頻道錄像 Three-Channel Video ｜ 2016

《巨神連線》系列攝影作品，拍攝全臺三百餘間廟宇、墓園、公園及樂園內一尊尊的巨大神像，主要關注漢人用自我形象所投射而形塑出來的神偶世界。透過這些信徒們的「巨大慾力」投射物，共構出臺灣地理空間內緊密交織的常民生活、信仰文化、與政治經濟關係，以宏觀的角度來呈現獨特的「規模美學」。

作品拍攝視角不若一般神像攝影意欲突顯神像莊嚴肅穆的神態，而是採用遠景將巨大神像座落的街廓與道路都一併攝入，有如行進中倏忽被超乎尋常的巨大神像吸引住目光，進而如實地以影像紀錄這些日常奇觀。三頻道錄像的大幅投影展示，將攝影影像更具震懾力，背景配樂為美國國家航空暨太空總署（NASA）錄製的宇宙聲響混合廟宇法會聲音，更是呈現出詭譎與魔幻的風格。

Incarnation is a photography series that features the monumental god statues in more than three hundred temples, cemeteries, public parks and amusement parks around Taiwan. The series reveals a world of religious iconography based on and shaped by the self-image of Han people. These objects, manifested by the religious followers' "powerful drives," have informed the folk life, religious culture and politico-economic relations intricately linked in the geographic space of Taiwan; and the series, with a macrocosmic view, displays an idiosyncratic "aesthetics of scale."

Unlike common god statue photography that tends to focus on the dignified, austere appearance of its subject, the artist utilizes wide shot to include the street environment surrounding these statues, foregrounding their extraordinary size that captures the eyes of passersby and realistically documenting these quotidian spectacles with his camera. The three-channel video projected on an enormous screen further elevates the photographic images to a state of grandeur. With the background music – a mixture of NASA's recording of cosmic sounds and that of religious festivals – the video immerses the audience in an eerie yet magical atmosphere.

GROUP
02

The Influential Relationship
Network Formed by
Socially Marginal Artists

第
02
組

社會邊緣人藝術家
自組具有影響力的
關係網絡

● Yi-Che, Chen
陳毅哲

Stargazing : 2014-2020
《觀星者：2014-2020》

複合媒材 Mixed Media │ 尺寸因空間而異 Dimensions Variable │ 2020

於 2014 年到 2016 年進駐淡水老街的閒置空間，經營展演空間「十八巷五號」。這棟建築物原是藥房，由於長年無人居住，藝術家為了使廢棄的空間恢復原有生活機能，持續與不同的社群合作展覽與活動，也逐漸建立起拓展的人際圖譜。直到搬遷到三重「天臺工作室」，這層網絡仍不斷地延伸。

展場內 100 多張拍立得拍攝的肖像，是藝術家於這兩個空間中，所往來認識的人際網絡，去除了真實的姓名後，他們被賦予一個編號，看似冷調的檔案紀錄，背後是各自想像與認知的身份背景，與彼此相遇及拍攝的時間空間跨度。藝術家藉由自身的藝術實踐，創造彼此相遇的契機，並重新串連起該空間場域的記憶。每個人在城市中都有如一顆恆星，有著自行運行的軌跡與體系，在某個偶然的時刻相互交織與相遇。

From 2014 to 2016, the artist resided a deserted space on the ancient street in Tamsui, and launched the exhibition space called "No.5 Lane 18 project." The building used to be a pharmacy but it had been disused at the period of time. Hence, its function had been repurposed through the cooperation of different communities to create exhibitions and events in all forms, gradually generating and expanding an interpersonal network. Even after the artist moved to "Rooftop Studio" in Sanchong, this network has continued growing.

On view in the exhibition are over 100 polaroid portraits that visualize the interpersonal network the artist has created between the two space. The artist replaces the real names of these people with a number. The seemingly cold archives somehow allow audiences to freely imagine and conceive the people's identities, backgrounds as well as the spatial and temporal dimensions of these encounters when these photographs were taken. To sum up, through his space practice, the artist has created opportunities for people's paths in life to cross and brought memories all back of the two spaces. Every urban dweller is like a shining star, orbiting around its own way in an individual system; that is until an unexpected, random moment of encounter arrives.

45

106

06

45

69

110

111

● Teng Wen Hsin
鄧雯馨

Murmur and Whisper
《牆角窸窣囈語》

錄像裝置 Video Installation │ 尺寸因空間而異 Dimensions Variable │ 2020

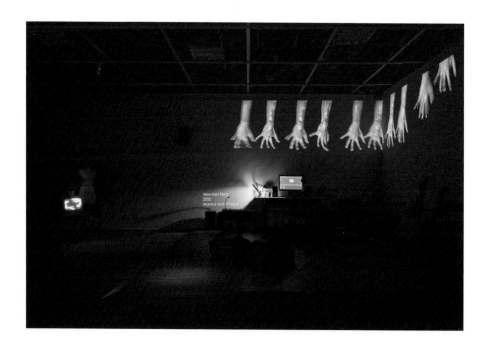

一如病毒需要宿主
像軟組織以血為食
有一天我會找到你，這迫切的慾望永存 —碧玉，「病毒」

輾轉難眠的夜裡，角落的灰塵、牆上正在生長的壁癌、與管線傳來的聲響，都傳出了細小微弱的聲音，彷彿房子正在發出不安的訊息。依附在房子的菌絲，在看不見之處逐漸蔓延，發出了看不見的聲響；人們生活在居所與城市之中，就有如病毒、黴菌、細菌般寄生在宿主身上，產生了相互影響的依附關係。

藝術家在 2016 年於臺北景美仙跡岩成立了「星空間」工作室，2 年後遷入了台北當代藝術館旁安靜巷弄，藉由不同的藝術與創作活動，在城市中串生了無數的關係網絡。這個作品中，藝術家重現了工作室的場景，透過聲音與影像裝置，於此空間交往的人們依附在這個空間宿主身上流動、蔓延、滲透，打破原有的樣貌，成長出迷幻的菌絲與觸角。幻麗的影像與聲音的互動中，打造一個可視場景，一層層互依存在的對話，於空間中共生。

Like a virus needs a body
As soft tissue feeds on blood
Some day I'll find you, the urge is here —Björk《Virus》

In those sleepless nights, the dust in the corners, the efflorescence growing on the walls and the pipelines behind the walls all seem to make faint, unclear sounds, as if the entire house is sending out unsettling messages. The fungal mycelia growing in the house are spreading across the unseen corners, making undetectable sounds. People dwelling in houses and cities are like viruses, mold and bacteria living off their hosts, creating a co-depending, symbiotic relationship.

In 2016, the artist founded her own studio "Hsin'Space" in Jingmei, Taipei. Two years later, the studio was moved to a quiet alley near MOCA Taipei. Through a wide range of art and creative events, Teng has established an ever-growing network of relations in the city. For this work, she recreates her studio, and uses sound and image installation to portray how the people visiting the space have attached themselves to the spatial host, flowing, spreading, permeating and changing the space's original look while growing psychedelic mycelia and tentacles. Through the mesmerizing, interacting image and sound, a visible scene is created, with interdependent dialogues coexisting, layer upon layer, in this space.

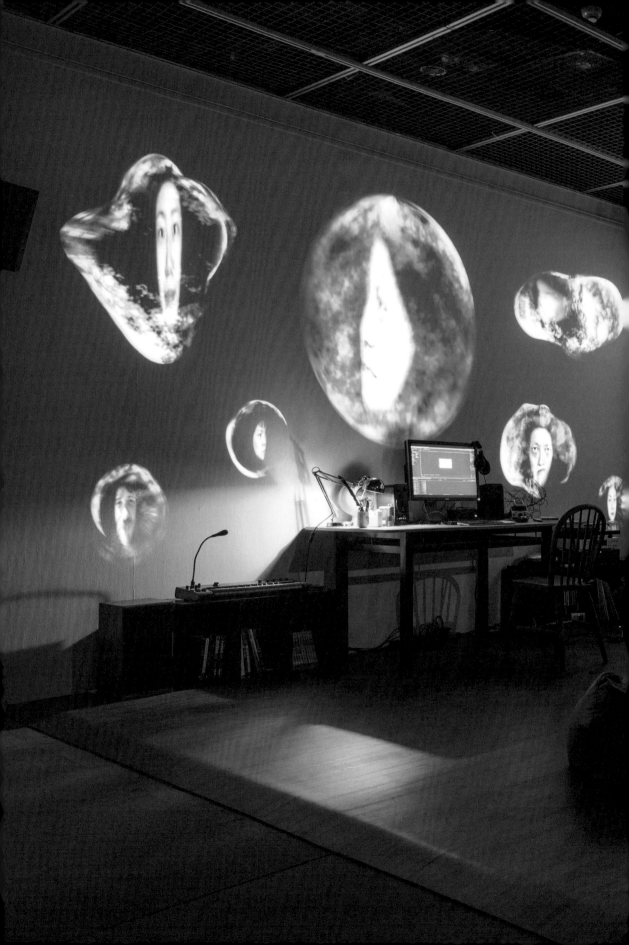

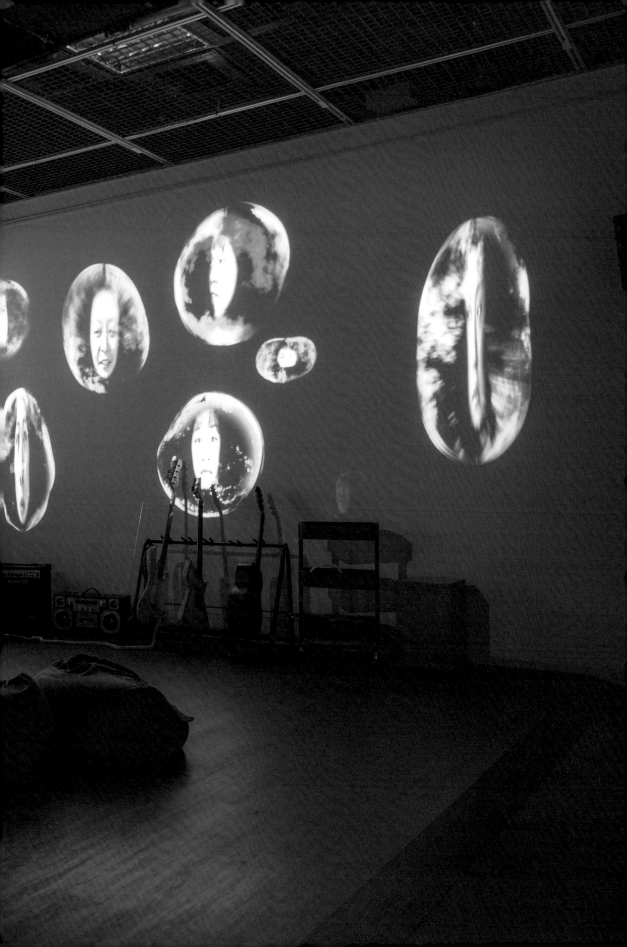

● LIN, Yi-Chi
林羿綺

Running Stitch – Bangkok
《運行針：曼谷》

雙頻道彩色有聲錄像 Duo-Channel Video, Color, Sound ｜ 8 min. ｜ 2017

《運行針：曼谷》是藝術家於泰國進行藝術創作駐村時的作品，針對那些屬於城市邊緣地帶的異質場域，進行一系列探訪地區神秘傳說的創作計劃。藝術家在泰國曼谷地區街頭隨意地進行游擊採訪，採集當地鬼魅與都市傳說等親身經歷，以「我在這裡沒有遇過靈魂，但是我有我的故事要說。」這句耐人尋味的句子，開啟了在曼谷艾縣 (Bangkok Yai)、孔提市場 (Khlong Toei Market)、華藍篷車站 (Hua Lamphong Station) 等三個不同區域的超自然經驗接續串連。

雙頻道的影像畫面，由當地人述說的故事字幕，輔以背景從雜訊中逐漸現身而又消逝的被訪問者肖像與事件發生地的動態影像相互並置。敘事性的文字與深具寓意的城市影像畫面相互串聯映照之後，就如同被正在運行的針來回穿梭，逐漸拓展並打破敘事裡的空間，重新尋找鍵結，進行一場影像與城市空間的拓樸實驗。

Created during an artist residency in Thailand, *Running Stitch – Bangkok* is a creative project involving investigating regional mysterious legends in heterogeneous sites of a city's peripheral areas. The artist conducted random, guerilla-style interviews on the streets of Bangkok, collecting personal experiences and stories about local supernatural existences and urban legends. Starting the interviews by beginning with an intriguing line – "I haven't met any spirits here, but I have my story to tell" – the work brings together supernatural experiences gathered from three areas in the city: Bangkok Yai, Khlong Toei Market and Hua Lamphong Station.

With subtitles narrating the locals' stories, the two-channel video juxtaposes slowly surfacing and then disappearing portraits of the interviewees and motion images of the locales where the stories have allegedly taken place. The narrative text and allegorical images of the city are interconnected and mutually referencing, which is reminiscent of a running stitch that gradually expands and breaks the narrative space while establishing new connections to unfold a topological experiment about image and urban space.

我不敢跟大人說，只好偷偷把抱枕丟到河裡去。
I didn't dare to tell adults
so that I secretly threw the pillow into a river.

ฉันไม่เคยเจอผีหรือวิญญาณที่นี่ แต่ฉันมีเรื่องราวของฉันจะเล่าให้ฟัง

我在這裏沒有遇過靈魂，但我有自己的故事要說。

I haven't met any spirits here, but I have my story to tell.

和尚說我前世害了人，
因果成熟時就會來找我討這筆債，

A monk said I did something harm to another person in my last
When the time came, he would come to me to get what I owned

เขตคลองเตย
KHLONG-TOEI COUNTY

孔堤市場

ตลาดท่าเรือ
PIER MARKET

我在這裏沒有遇過靈魂，但是我有我的故事要說。

haven't met any spirits here, but I have my story to tell.

เขต ปทุมวัน่
PATHUM WAN COUNTY

華藍蓬車站

หัวลำโพง
HUA LAMPHONG STATION

● Tang Tang-Fa + FIDATI (PINDY WINDY)
唐唐發 ＋ FIDATI (PINDY WINDY)

Indonesian Grocery Store in Taiwan
《印尼雜貨店在台灣》

空間裝置 Installation ｜ 尺寸因空間而異 Dimensions Variable ｜ 2020

因應越來越多散居臺灣各地印尼移工和新住民的需求，城市及鄉間興起許多印尼雜貨店，這些總位於不起眼角落的商店不僅提供了印尼獨有和清真認證的食材、香料等商品，也是當地印尼朋友聚會甚至進行宗教儀式的地方，這些雜貨店超越了商業交易行為的場所功能，成為了離鄉背井者維繫情感及延續文化傳統的聚集地。

唐唐發與 FIDATI (PINDY WINDY) 的《印尼雜貨店在台灣》所陳列看似一件件的商品，都是在臺印尼人所帶來與家鄉、家人連結的物品，這些物品已不再是提供消費的商品，而是乘載著情感與生活文化習慣的物件。其中印尼文化題材的捏麵人作品，為 PINDY 擔任看護期間因緣際會學成的捏麵人手藝；印尼皮影戲偶則是唐唐發根據《羅摩衍那》故事所繪製而成。在這些物品背後所蘊含的情感與文化交流價值之下，這間雜貨店也成為了臺灣民眾認識在臺印尼人的櫥窗。

Due to the increasing demand for Indonesian immigrant workers and new residents around Taiwan, there has been a growing number of Indonesian grocery stores in both Taiwan's urban and rural areas. These stores are usually inconspicuous, not only offering unique halal food and ingredients from Indonesia but also serving as venues for Indonesians in Taiwan to meet up and even perform religious rituals. In truth, these grocery stores have surpassed their commercial functions, and emerged as hubs for those from Indonesia to socialize and continue their cultural tradition.

Tang Tang-Fa and FIDATI (PINDY WINDY) create *Indonesian Grocery Store in Taiwan*, which displays a number of objects that connect the Indonesians in Taiwan with their hometowns and families. These objects are no longer products waiting for consumers; instead, they carry people's sentiments as well as living and cultural customs. Among the objects, the dough figurines embodying Indonesian cultural themes were created by Pindy, who learned this craft when she was working as a caregiver. The Indonesian shadow puppets were created by Tang Tang-Fa based on the epic, *Ramayana*. With the sentiments and value of cultural exchange symbolized by these objects, this grocery store is in truth a window for the audience to gain a deeper understanding of the Indonesians in Taiwan and their life here.

Varied Species Moving and
Working at Different Altitude and Speed

第
03
組

以不同高度、
速度運動及
工作的物種

● Deng Yau-Horng
鄧堯鴻

Shadow of a Cocoon 《繭影》
塑鋼、玻璃纖維 Fiber Reinforced Plastics ｜ 380 x 120 x 120 cm ｜ 2016-2018

Remainder and Green 《剩餘與蔥翠》
複合媒材 Mixed Media ｜ 尺寸因空間而異 Dimensions Variable ｜ 1993-2019

「一個形體尋覓一個容積，一個輕盈承載一個量感，在囹圄中有了開始──」

鄧堯鴻將老家角落已發臭的老鼠乾屍撿拾起來，反轉成巨大的雕塑作品─《繭影》，逝去的老鼠潰爛破敗在陰暗之處，找尋不到形體，但腐敗的氣味卻依舊宣示著曾經的存在，始終徘徊不去。從展場二樓垂直懸吊貫穿至一樓入口處的巨大老鼠，彷彿仍欲奔馳著穿穴逾牆，身軀卻早已乾枯，只剩殘破的軀殼。觀者視線貫穿這個軀殼，連結至彼方。眾生皮相與慾望僅為虛幻之物，作繭自縛罷了。

《剩餘與蒽翠》作品中，鄧堯鴻收集不同的剩餘與廢棄之物，對他來說餘光、餘地、餘步、餘波、餘燼，每一餘態皆有其習性，殘餘與殘缺原本就是生命的本質，在這樣的不完整與不確定的狀態下，反而具備了可塑的因子。因此他將生活中俯拾即是的微小與脆弱的殘片重新組裝，將腐朽之物賦予新生。

A form seeks a vessel; the lightness bears a sense of volume; in imprisonment, the beginning emerges—

Deng Yau-Horng collected the stinky, desiccated rats found in his old home, and turned them into a monumental sculptural installation—*Shadow of a Cocoon*. The dead rats decomposed in the shadow; and whereas the artist had a hard time finding where they had perished, the putrid odor of rotting rats lingered and proclaimed its presence. This enormous rat suspended from the 2nd-floor gallery room and on view in the 1st-floor entrance space reminds the audience a rat that is still trying to run through holes in walls. Nevertheless, its body has withered into a broken shell, or what is left of it. The audience can see through the crevices on its body, seemingly connecting with "the other side." The physical appearances of all living creatures as well as desires are in truth illusions that bind and confine us.

Remainder and Green is created with a myriad of leftover items and scraps collected by the artist. For Deng, whatever the residue is – be it light, space, movement, waves, embers – it manifests its distinctive qualities. Residues and lacks make up the nature of life; and it is in this incomplete and uncertain state that life becomes moldable. Therefore, he reconstructs the insignificant and fragile fragments that can be found everywhere in daily life, breathing a new life to the decay.

● Huang Yen-Chao
黃彥超

Food Winger

四頻道影像、四軌聲音多媒體影音裝置
4-Channel Video, 4-Tracks Sounds Multimedia Installation ｜ 2020

「行動送餐」是近年來迅速興起的新型態消費模式，不僅讓消費者與餐廳間的交易網絡更加擴展且快速地流動，穿梭於大街小巷的外送員也逐步改變了城市的景觀，擔任起串聯起整個網絡的主體。然而在藝術家與外送員訪談的過程中，卻發現了更多關於資本制度下的生存、消費、勞動的矛盾與掙扎，以及身體感的陌生化與工具化。

藝術家將外送員每日移動的 Google Map 路徑作為發想點，揣想外送員每日移動範圍的日常繞圈行為，有如一場出不去的感性迴圈。影像中穿著全白服裝及外送背包的女子，被去除了符號與身份，漫無目的地溜著滑板或滑著手機，彷彿在等待一個契機或是尋找一個出口。街景的畫面如影隨形地投影在女子身上，像在操控、導航著她的行動，伴隨著忽遠忽近的口白與尖銳嘈雜的電子聲響，她就有如展間大量製造的塑膠小鳥玩具影像，不斷地繞圈振翅旋轉，卻無法自由翱翔。

"Food delivery" is one of the emerging consumption modes in recent years, which not only expands the trade network between consumers and restaurants, increasing its rapid flow, but also slowly changes the cityscape with the food deliverers, or food wingers, moving swiftly through streets and alleyways in cities. These food deliverers collectively form the core of this network. However, during the artist's interviews with them, more and more conflicts and struggles underlying the survival, consumption and labor in the capitalist system begin to surface, along with the alienation and instrumentalization of the body.

The artist draws inspiration from the food deliverers' daily routes from Google Maps, and reimagines their everyday activity as running in circles, forming a series of loops that permit no escape. In the video, the woman in white with a delivery sack is stripped of any symbols and identity, aimlessly wandering on her skateboard or swiping her phone, as if she is waiting for an opportunity or seeking an exit. The streetscape is projected on the woman's body, seemingly monitoring and guiding her movement anywhere she goes. Along with the indistinct narration and piercing, noisy electronic sound, the woman seems to become one of the mass-produced plastic birds in the videos on view in the same gallery room, flapping the wings and flying in circle without ever being able to enjoy freedom.

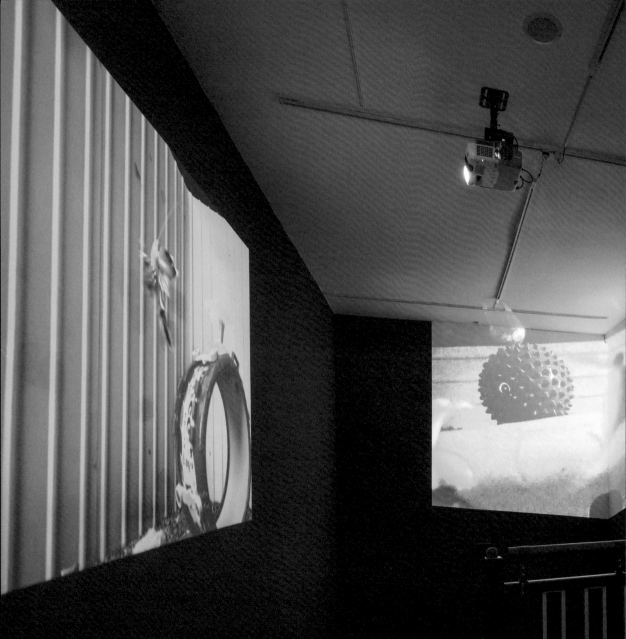

● HSU, HUI-CHING
許惠晴

Border Roaming
《邊境漫遊》

雙頻道錄像 Duo-Channel Video ｜ 2020

許惠晴曾擔任過空服員，不斷地離開地平線並穿梭往來於各國邊境，在機場、機艙、旅館等不具歸屬感的「非地方」間移動。處於這些熟悉卻帶著陌生感的場景之中，身體彷彿失去了與周遭環境的連結，但肉身的存有空間卻益發顯得真實。然而，「空服員」的身份在性別建構、階級分層與資本消費下，承載了許多偏見與刻板印象，這些僵化的桎梏讓她失去了話語權，只能無聲地執行被賦予的角色。

一樓走廊的影像，藝術家戴著口罩穿著航空制服，口腔反覆咀嚼食物並噴射出去，象徵失語卻仍渴求自我表述的狀態，圈構出強烈的、碎形的、抽象的、隱晦的繽紛風景，直射觀者眼底，彷彿在對抗展間樓梯上方影像所呈現出順服的空姐形象。影片中空姐在客艙中像個乖順的演員，服膺著他人賦予的詮釋與觀看，以主動或被動的變裝模式不停更衣，呈現出社會的、文化的、政治的、性別的身體景觀。

HSU, HUI-CHING used to be a flight attendant, whose work took her over the horizon, travelling through borders and moving between "non-places" such as airports, aircraft cabins and hotels. Finding herself in these familiar yet strange settings, her body becomes disconnected with the surrounding environment, whereas her corporeal space of being seems to become more real. However, the identity of "flight attendant" is structured by gender construction, social class and capitalist consumerism, and is consequently stereotyped with many prejudices. The rigid restriction has cost her right to speech, and under such circumstance, she could only silently perform the role she was assigned.

In the video work showing on the 1st-floor hallway, the artist is wearing a facial mask and an airline uniform while chewing food in her mouth spitting it out repeatedly—a symbol of losing her voice yet longing to express herself. An intense, fragmented, abstract, ambiguous landscape is constructed and imprinted in the mind of the audience, creating a force of resistance against the submissive image of a female flight attendant displayed above the stairway. In the video upstairs, the female flight attendant, playing her docile role, conforms to other's interpretation and gaze. Whether actively or passively, she keeps changing her outfit to reveal the social, cultural, political and genderized body.

Returning to the
Inescapable Haze of
History?

第
04
組

難以掙脫
歷史迷障的
回歸？

● Liang Ting-Yu
梁廷毓

The Capturing River
《襲奪之河》

錄像裝置 Video Installation ｜ 尺寸因空間而異 Dimensions Variable ｜ 2020

《襲奪之河》是由〈圖誌：Mutu〉、〈脊谷〉、〈襲奪河〉、與〈問石〉組成的影像裝置。〈圖誌：Mutu〉中呈現桃園大溪、龍潭、復興與新竹關西一帶，過去原、漢衝突頻繁的的四方交界之處，以泰雅族部落 Mutu（今關西馬武督一帶）的視角，紀錄清末時由山脊至山谷捍衛傳統社域的獵首路徑，勾勒出因當地地形與地質條件觸發的死亡地景，以及地點的命名所透露出的過去地方歷史。

〈脊谷〉與〈襲奪河〉則從原、客族群雙方耆老的交叉敘事中，追溯昔日發生衝突的死亡地點、親族記憶、無頭鬼與石爺傳說。相關的靈異經驗、詛咒、與屍首掩埋之處，讓過往的死亡恐懼依舊徘徊縈繞在地方記憶與地景之中，形成了一個共享於族群雙方的深層記憶與泛靈宇宙相互交疊的地域。〈問石〉由自然溝通師與相傳曾在原、客衝突中保護客家人的石爺對話，將跨越人類主體的神靈視角納入地方誌的書寫之中。

The Capturing River is a video installation comprising Cartography: Mutu, The Ridge and the Valley, Blood Flows in Rivers and The Cartography of Stone. Cartography: Mutu displays the border area among Taoyuan's Daxi, Longtan, Fuxing and Hsinchu's Guanxi, which was informed by historical conflicts between the indigenous community and the Han people. From the perspective of the Atayal tribe Mutu (now the area of Guanxi's Mawudu), the work documents the headhunting trail extending from the mountain ridge to the valley at the end of Qing dynasty, and delineates the ominous landscape, deadly due to the topography and geological condition as well as the local history revealed by the name of the place.

The Ridge and the Valley and Blood Flows in Rivers trace back to the locales of fatal conflicts in the past, revisit family memory and bring up legends of headless ghouls and "Shiye" (literally stone father) from the interweaving narratives told by elders in indigenous and Hakka communities. Related supernatural experiences, curses and burial places sustain the lingering fear of death in local memory and landscape, forming a site where the communities' distant memory and the pantheistic cosmos overlap. The Cartography of Stone revolves around the dialogue between a nature communicator and Shiye – the legendary protector of Hakka people in the conflicts between the indigenous and Hakka communities – and incorporates the supernatural perspective surpassing human subject into the writing of chorography.

就不知道怎麼樣⋯兩個就在河邊⋯
Nobody knew how... the two of them at the river...

● ZHANG XU zhan
張徐展

《Si So Mi》

錄像裝置 Video Installation ｜ 尺寸因空間而異 Dimensions Variable ｜ 2017-2018

臺灣人因避諱談論死亡，早期常以 Si So Mi 稱呼喪葬儀隊，這三個音實際上源於西樂隊傳自臺灣時，所流行的一首德國愛情歌曲「Ach wie ist's möglich dann（我怎能離開你）」。因為這個有趣的文化轉譯，張徐展將歌曲翻唱後，以舊報紙將城市角落中那些卑微、汙穢、避之唯恐不及的生命紮成戲偶，以各種城市生存的死亡事故，編織了一支歡慶與荒誕交織而成的舞蹈。

影片中乾扁的老鼠戴上繽紛的生日派對帽，望著鏡中的自我，回顧自身生命歷程；喪葬儀隊為眾多無名亡靈進行歡樂地演奏；歌舞團將老鼠被人類驅趕、遭黏鼠器捕捉、溺水等卑賤的生存經驗轉換成一場舞蹈狂歡，有如一種自我解嘲的黑色幽默，也是一場儀式，將生存與死亡的荒謬與孤寂，轉化為永不間斷的慶典。透過觀點的挪移，創造了有如中陰身的渾沌空間，將生與死、自我與他者、崇高與卑賤、純淨與汙穢之間中過渡。

Death has been somewhat a taboo that most Taiwanese people prefer to avoid. In the earlier days, people referred to funeral bands with the nickname, "Si So Mi"— three musical notes that in fact originated from a sorrowful German love song, "Ach wie ist's möglich dann" (Oh how's that possible then), which was popular when the Western funeral band was introduced into Taiwan. Based on this fascinating cultural translation, ZHANG XU zhan recorded the song and used old newspaper to turn puny, filthy and outcast lives in urban corners into paper figures. Drawing inspiration from various death accidents commonly heard in a city, the artist choreographed a festive and absurd dance.

In the video, the desiccated rats are wearing colorful party hats, looking into their reflection in the mirror while taking a backward glance on their lives. The funeral procession band is joyfully playing music for countless souls that have departed from this world. The music band converts the rats' humble living experiences – being chased by humans, captured by glue traps, drowned, etc. – into a carnivalesque dance with the quality of self-mocking black humor as well as a rite that transforms the absurdity and solitude of survival and death into a never-ending celebration. By appropriating existing perspectives, the artist creates a liminal space of the intermediate state in the afterlife, and portrays the transition between life to death, self and other, the superior and the inferior as well as the pure and the filthy.

疫情不在的時候你也從沒愛過我。
Even prior to the Covid-19, you have never loved me.

● Yan Chung-Hsien
顏忠賢

Hell
《地獄變相》

複合媒材裝置 Multi-media Installation ｜ 尺寸因空間而異 Dimensions Variable ｜ 2020

本作品是從藝術家即將發行的小說《地獄變相》所發展出來，有如一種老調又帶著自嘲、怪異又帶著恐慌的軟建築式地獄殿。顏忠賢引用唐朝畫聖吳道子繪製的《地獄變相》古壁畫及十殿閻羅古圖，呈現閻王判官、牛頭馬面、鬼兵鬼卒，及兩側長幅書法畫軸「人惡人怕天不怕，人善人欺天不欺」的勸世句，神威震攝如醮典般地陰森排場；滿地如眾生相般的小鬼頭，則有如在夜市插電亂動、鬼吼鬼叫、群魔亂舞的動力裝置，打造出一個在臺灣民間遊地府的偽殘酷劇場。

同時展出的小說也與本作品互為隱喻：一個陰陽眼 / 庫官 / 廟公 / 策展人找了三十六個觀落陰等級的鬼藝術家來做出「地獄變相」千年大展。作品也一如小說中總是糾纏不清的藝術家，最終變成鬼頭鬼腦的恐怖份子般地，以殺人來救人、以滅世來淑世地體現「人間就是地獄」悖論，然而恐怖感總不免就是喜感，終究可怕又可笑地撐起一齣當代荒誕劇場。

Hell is derived from the artist's upcoming homonymous novel and reveals a traditional, self-mocking, grotesque and terrifying court of the underworld in the form of soft architecture. Yan draws inspiration from the ancient, similarly themed mural and the painting of hell palaces by the Tang art master, Wu Tao-Tzu, and creates an impressive, ceremonious scene of hell, with its judge king, ox-head and horse-face guardians, ghoul soldiers and two calligraphic scrolls on both sides of the court that read, "Bad men are feared but not by heaven. Good men might be bullied but not by heaven." The ground is covered by heads of tiny ogres, which bring to mind common mechanical apparatuses in Taiwanese night markets that, once plugged in, would show wiggling and screaming puppets, creating a pseudo theater of cruelty that gives people a glimpse of hell.

The novel on view in the exhibition, in a similar way, serves as a metaphorical reference to the work: the clairvoyant/vault protector/temple host/curator invites thirty-six ghost artists from hell to produce a grand exhibition themed on the various manifestations of the underworld. Like the haunting artists in the novel, their works eventually surface as entangling, ghastly creations that promulgate the paradoxical idea that resembles terrorism—to save by killing and to redeem the world by destroying it, their works embody the statement, "this world is nothing but a living hell." However, the extremely terrifying sometimes appears ridiculously comical, and the hell of horror eventually becomes a theater of absurdity beckoning the contemporary reality.

● KUO I-Chen
郭奕臣

That's One Small Step for Mankind, One Giant Leap for Species
《這是人類的一小步，物種的一大步》

複合媒材 Mixed Media ｜ 尺寸因空間而異 Dimensions Variable ｜ 2019-2020

NASA 宣佈將在 2024 年重返月球，人類登月已超過半世紀，生存的競爭與超越極限的慾望引領人類不斷實驗前進，人類作為眾多物種之一，以科技進行自我演化，從平視、俯視、進而發展出了太空視角。本作品試圖研究物種在面對各種極端與過渡的狀態下，所產生的對抗與演化歷程，以及科技的輔佐下所造成物種與物種間的變異生存狀態。

201 展間中，結合了始祖鳥圖樣、拍攝人類首次登月的哈蘇相機、與米格 15 戰機座椅的機械裝置，彷彿即將從階梯上登陸進行演化；鴿舍中放置了不同物種在生存對抗與過渡轉化的文件，包含孤雌繁殖的突變物種－大理石紋螯蝦、用於戰爭空中偵察的的鴿子攝影、始祖鳥象徵人類從爬行類過渡到鳥類的太空競賽，對比廣場上觀眾登上螺旋梯後，見到的廢棄中央通訊社員工宿舍[1] 檔案照，以及電視牆上閃現首架米格 15 戰機投奔自由墜毀畫面；這每一步彷彿都在追尋一個近烏托邦的「登月」行動，究竟會引領人類與物種踏上甚麼樣的未來？

It has been over half a century since human beings first landed on the moon when NASA announced the plan to return to the moon in 2024. The competition for survival and limitless desires have driven humanity to continuously experiment and progress. As one of the animal species, human beings have self-evolved through technology, and moved from a horizontal view, to an aerial view to a space view. Through this work, the artist attempts to study the resistance and evolution of species as well as the technology-induced mutation existing between species under extreme and transitional circumstances.

In Room 201, the installation brings together image of archaeopteryx, the Hasselblad used to photograph humanity's first landing on the moon and the mechanical device of the pilot seat in the MiG-15, suggesting an evolution starting from stepping onto the stairway. In the pigeon house are documents displaying various species' fight for survival and transitional transformation, such as marbled crayfish that has mutated to carry out parthenogenesis, pigeon photography used in reconnaissance, and archaeopteryx as a symbol for humanity's transition from reptiles to birds, and finally, the space competition. In comparison to the archival images of the disused staff dormitory of the Central News Agency[1] that the audience sees when climbing unto the spiral staircase on the plaza and the image of a crashed MiG 15 after its deflection to freedom showing on the plaza's LED screen, every step of mankind is part of a quasi-utopian quest of "moon-landing," a quest into a future that no human beings nor any other species could foresee.

1.
本作品為「實踐街 1 號登月計畫」的階段性呈現，計畫原定藝術家以臺北市實踐街 1 號的廢棄中央通訊社員工宿舍進行創作與研究，然而該建築於 2020 年四月已然面臨拆除命運。
This work is a phased presentation of "Shijian St. 1 Landing Program," which was originally planned to be conducted and carried out in the disused staff dormitory of the Central News Agency at No. 1, Shijian Street in Taipei City; however, the building was demolished in April 2020.

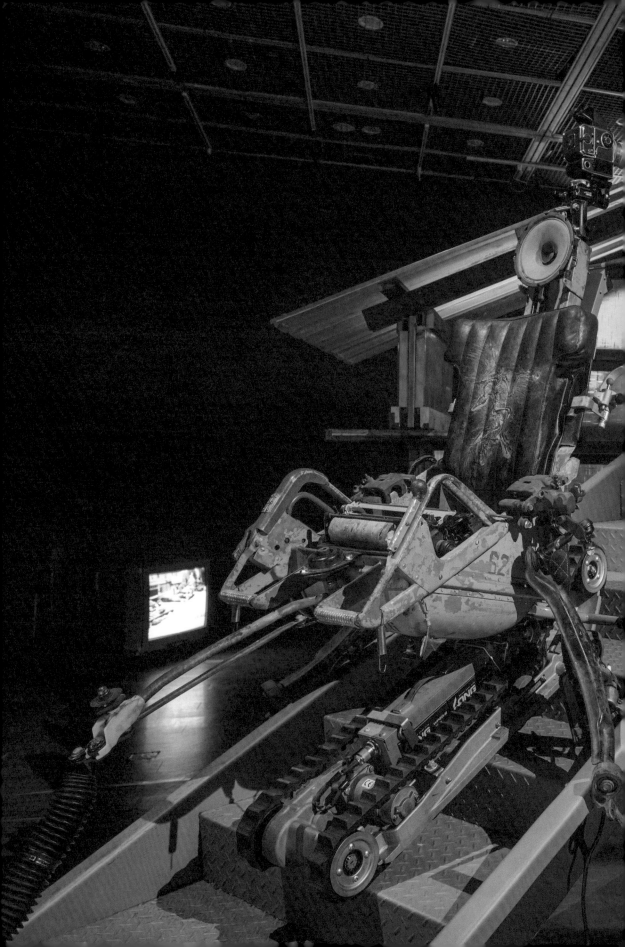

● WU Yi-Hua
吳宜樺

Inside-out D-scène
《裡外急轉彎的D場景 》

複合媒材裝置 Mixed Media Installation │ 尺寸因空間而異 Dimensions Variable │ 2020

乍看像是某個熟悉的日常生活中的場景，近看卻發現這些物件彷彿遭到一場突如其來的災難，如化石般倏忽凍結而被快速質變轉換成為水泥體，這些物件被藝術家以細微而荒謬的並列形式結合在一起，在構成上處理了重量、質感、顏色、形狀和紋理之間的相互作用，就像一個集合各種形狀和表面／介面物件的星象體，彼此間保留生動活潑的獨立形式，但又緊密地結合在一起。部分物件也被以螢綠色塊塗裝的方式轉化為反物件（anti-object），以綠幕特效的手法，在錄像中將物件的形象合成上高度流動性的影像，異轉成白板（*tabula rasa*）狀態：無止無盡地快速再置入與更新事物間的次序。藝術家以德國劇作家海納・穆勒（Heiner Müller）的《哈姆雷特機器》作為構思的靈感藍圖，藉著這個影像幻術、藝術性的空間佈局和材質功能的交錯推拉，影射當代數位文化裡大量氾濫的合成影像景觀如何穿透我們的日常感官，呈現人工智慧時代下被風化的消費文化景觀與當代人存有經驗的極端虛構性。

At first glance, the work is reminiscent of a certain familiar scene in daily life; but a closer look reveals that these objects seem to have emerged from a disastrous scene and have instantly become concrete fossils through a qualitative change. These objects are arranged and combined by the artist in a delicate yet absurd way. The composition reveals an interaction between weight, texture, color, form and pattern, forming a galactic constellation of a wide range of forms and surfaces/interface objects that retain their lively, unique formations but still intricately connect with each other. Some objects are painted neon green and turned into anti-objects before they are altered into a *tabula rasa* (blank slate) in the video, in which their images are composited with highly fluid images, creating an endless, rapid re-placement and renewal of the order of things. Wu is inspired by *Hamlet Machine* written by German playwright Heiner Müller. With illusory images, artistically configured space as well as interlacing and interchanging materials and functions, the work signals how the landscape of mass composited images in contemporary digital culture has penetrated our daily senses, revealing the eroded landscape of consumer culture as well as the extreme fictionality that informs contemporary people's experience of being.

● Kuo Yu-Ping
郭俞平

There Is a Light That Enters Houses With No Other House In Sight
《一盞燈進入房子，看不到其他房子 》

空間裝置 Space Installation ｜ 尺寸因空間而異 Dimensions variable ｜ 2020

這個含括了多重的錄像、聲音與物件，有如劇場般的空間裝置，看起來像是正在裝修中，又像早已被棄置，有種曖昧不明又難以界定的狀態。這個被藝術家建造起來，巍巍顫顫又脆弱不安的房子，象徵著對個人依歸的烏托邦願景之無盡追尋，然而似乎尚未落成，就已先擱置，成為廢墟。

展間的三部影片，儀隊有如幽靈般不斷地踏步，像是存在於潛意識晦暗不明的國族意念，依舊在內心深處纏繞不去；蒐集而來的家電被藝術家暴力地逐一敲碎；筆直的大道旁，是灰暗的模組化現代大樓，大道的遠方看不到盡頭。無數的家庭廢棄產品和包裝，被敲碎、剪裁、重新製作為彷彿戰爭的廢墟。藝術家試圖藉此勾勒出國族想像以及戰爭對現代性發展的影響，及其如何滲入家庭與意識，成為去殖民主體的深層欲望，甚至是主體構成的核心概念—「一個人不能不去想要的」，猶如一種現代人的精神官能症、薛西弗斯的徒勞。

This theatrical space installation comprising multiple videos, sound and objects looks like a space that is still under construction or a long abandoned place in an indeterminate, ambiguous state. The disconcertingly shaky, fragile house constructed by the artist symbolizes one's eternal quest for the utopian vision. However, before the vision can be realized, it seems to have been shelved and fallen into a ruinous state.

On view in the room are three videos. One shows honor guards repeating their steps in a ghost-like manner, bringing to mind the ambiguous national ideology forever lurking and haunting in one's subconscious in the deep corner of the mind. In another one, the artist is violently smashing gathered home appliances one after another. The other video reveals a perfectly straight boulevard, seemingly extending endlessly, with gloomy looking, modularized multi-story buildings lining up on both sides. Countless discarded home products and packaging materials are shattered, cut and reconstructed into a post-war ruin. Through this work, the artist delineates national imagination, the impact of wars on the development of modernity, and how they have infiltrated families and minds to shape the deepest desire of the decolonized subject and even formulate the core concept of the subject—"a person cannot stop wanting," which is a schizophrenic symptom of modern people as well as futility embodied by Sisyphus's story.

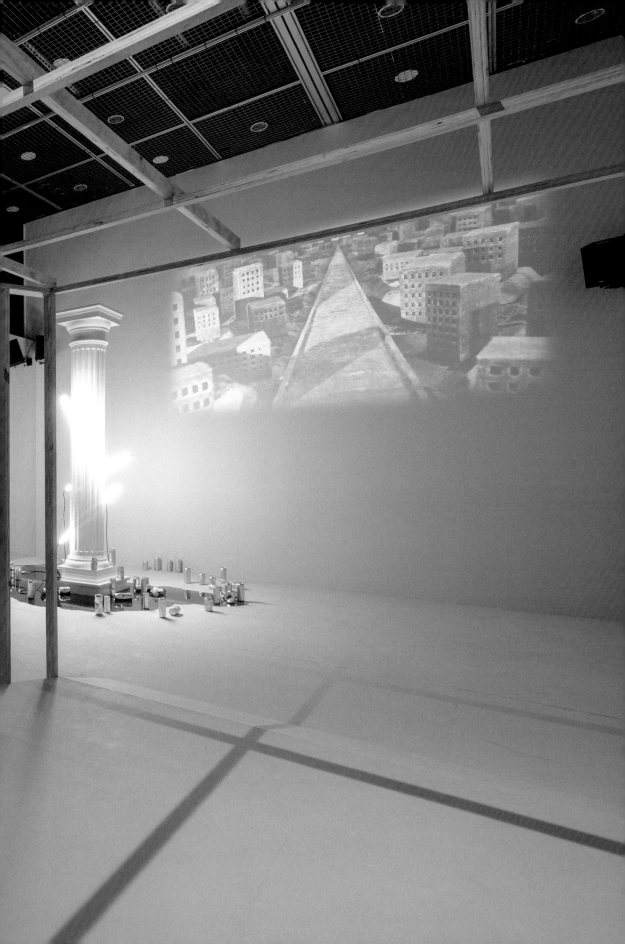

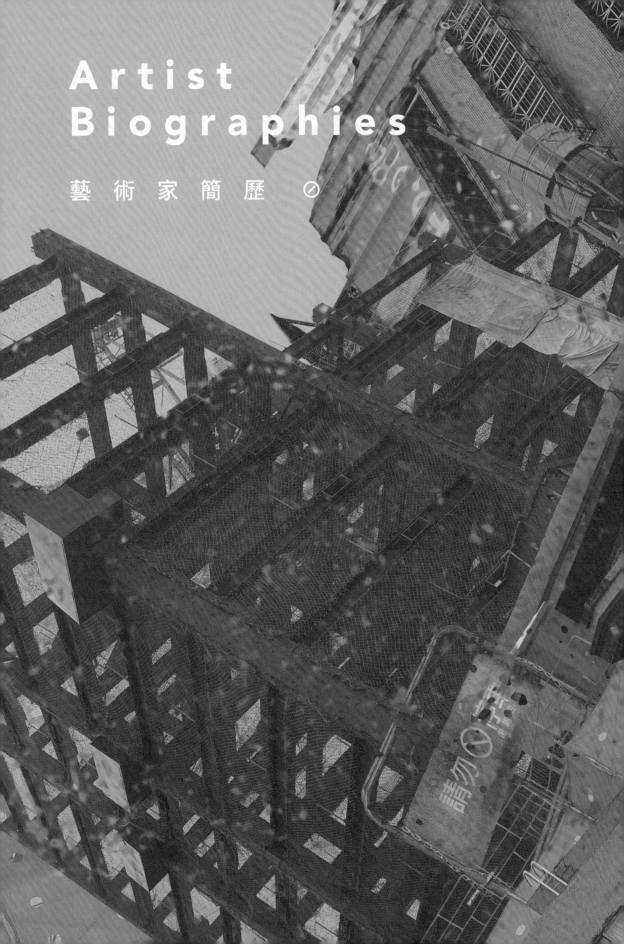

Artist
Biographies

藝術家簡歷 ⊘

朱駿騰 Chu ChunTeng

學歷
2010 英國倫敦金匠大學藝術創作碩士

節選個展
2020「來去匆匆—朱駿騰個展」，關渡美術館，臺北，臺灣
2019「天台—朱駿騰個展」，台北當代藝術館，臺北，臺灣
2017「八月十五」，洪建全文教基金會，覓空間，臺北，臺灣
2016「原地打轉」，Tong Gallery + Projects，北京，中國
2012「我叫小黑—朱駿騰個展」，視盟藝文空間，臺灣

節選聯展
2020「臺北美術獎」，臺北市立美術館，臺北，臺灣
2020「禽獸不如—2020 臺灣美術雙年展」，國立臺灣美術館，
　　　臺中，臺灣
2014「台北雙年展—劇烈加速度」，臺北市立美術館，臺北，臺灣
2012「我從我的小眼睛監視著」，埃森當代美術館，埃森，德國
2012「移動中的邊界」，荷茲利亞當代藝術中心，荷茲利亞，以色列

Education
2010　MFA in Fine Art, Goldsmiths, University of London,
　　　London, UK

Selected Solo Exhibitions
2020　"And It Came to Pass — Chu ChunTeng Solo Exhibition",
　　　Kuandu Museum of Fine Arts, Taipei, Taiwan
2019　"Rooftop - ChuChunTeng Solo exhibition", MOCA Taipei,
　　　Taipei, Taiwan
2017　"Parallel", Hung Foundation MEME Space, Taipei, Taiwan
2016　"Idling", Tong Gallery+Projects, Beijing, China
2012　"My Name is Little Black—Chu ChunTeng solo
　　　exhibition", Association of the Visual Arts, Taipei, Taiwan

Selected Group Exhibitions
2020　"Taipei Art Awards", Taipei Fine Art Museum, Taipei,
　　　Taiwan
2020　"Subzoology: 2020 Taiwan Biennial", National Taiwan
　　　Museum of Fine Arts, Taichung, Taiwan
2014　"Taipei Biennial- The Great Acceleration", Taipei Fine
　　　Art Museum, Taiwan
2012　"I SPY WITH MY LITTLE EYE", Kunsthaus Essen, Essen,
　　　Germany
2012　"Boundaries on the Move: Taiwan –Israel, a Cross-
　　　culture Dialogue", Herzliya Museum of Contemporary
　　　Art, Herzliya, Israel

吳宜樺 WU Yi-Hua

1978 年出生於臺灣嘉義市。創作研究取向喜好超越單一歷史軸線的
學科中心主義，透過多向量的感知框架在學科邊際上游移某種「不規
矩」，與不同領域的藝術家們一起實驗藝術化學的火花，在當代藝術
及當代表演藝術之間進行實驗性策略的發明。

目前任職國立臺灣藝術大學美術系助理教授，擁有法國巴黎第八大學
美學、科學與藝術科技博士文憑、法國巴黎國家高等裝飾藝術學院互
動藝術後文憑（Post-diplôme）。

As an artist, WU Yi-Hua has conducted several performative
projects in the form of new media installation and trans-
disciplinary collaborations. What characterizes her is a non-
disciplinary work and a method of collaboration with different
people, using a game-structure: each person is alternately
director / author and performer for the other one.

WU Yi-Hua teaches at the Department of Fine Arts in the
National Taiwan University of Arts since 2017. She graduated
with a PhD in Aesthetics, Science and Technologies of the
Arts from University Paris VIII in 2014 and a Postgraduate
Diploma from the École Nationale Supérieure des Arts
Décoratifs in Paris. Her research focuses on the fields of new
media, of performance studies and practices.

林羿綺 LIN, Yi-Chi

學歷

目前就讀國立臺灣藝術大學電影系碩士班

2016 畢業於國立臺北藝術大學美術系碩士班

2010 畢業於國立臺灣藝術大學雕塑學系

個展

2020 「越洋信使」，鳳甲美術館，臺北，臺灣

2017 「琥珀之夢」，福利社，臺北，臺灣

2016 「穿越回歸線」，水谷藝術，臺北，臺灣

節選聯展

2020 「綠島人權藝術季—如果，在邊緣，畫一個座標」，綠島，臺灣

2019 「日惹雙年展」，Jogja Contemporary，日惹特區，印尼

2019 「情書·手繭·後戰爭」，關渡美術館，臺北，臺灣

2018 「臺北美術獎」，臺北市立美術館，臺北，臺灣

2018 「高雄獎」，高雄市立美術館，高雄市，臺灣

Education

Currently studying in the Department of Motion Picture, National Taiwan University of Arts

2016 MFA, Department of Fine Arts School of Fine Arts, Taipei National University of the Arts

2010 BFA, Department of Sculpture School of Fine Arts, National Taiwan University of Arts

Solo exhibitions

2020 "Selamat, the messenger over the sea", Hong-gah Museum, Taipei, Taiwan

2017 "Dream of Amber", FreeS Art Space, Taipei, Taiwan

2016 "Across the Tropic of Cancer", Waley Art, Taipei, Taiwan

Selected Group Exhibitions

2020 "Green Island Human Rights Art Festival - If on the margin, draw a coordinate", Green Island, Taiwan

2019 "Biennale Jogja - Bilik Taiwan", Jogja contemporary, Yogyakarta, Indonesia

2019 "Letter · Callus · Post-war", Kuandu Museum of Fine Arts, Taipei, Taiwan

2018 "Taipei Art Awards", Taipei Fine Arts Museum, Taipei, Taiwan

2018 "Kaohsiung Award", Kaohsiung Museum of Fine Arts, Kaohsiung, Taiwan

---

姚瑞中 YAO Jui Chung

學歷

1994 畢業於國立臺北藝術大學美術系

節選個展

2020 「犬儒共和國」，臺灣當代藝術實驗室，臺北，臺灣

2017 「巨神連線」，TKG+，臺北，臺灣

2014 「從迷走到見證：姚瑞中前蚊子館影像紀事展」，威尼斯建築雙年展，義大利

2006 「所有一切都將成為未來的廢墟」，臺北市立美術館，臺北，臺灣

1997 「反攻大陸行動—預言篇 & 行動篇」，帝門藝術教育基金會，臺北，臺灣

節選聯展

2018 「上海雙年展」，Switch Art Center，上海，中國

2016 「雪梨雙年展」，Carriageworks，雪梨，澳洲

2009 「亞太當代藝術三年展」，昆士蘭美術館，布里斯班，澳洲

2005 「橫濱三年展：藝術馬戲團—跳躍日常」，橫濱，日本

1997 「威尼斯雙年展 / 臺灣·臺灣—面目全非」，威尼斯，義大利

Education

1994 BA, Art Theory, Taipei National University of the Arts

Selected Solo Exhibitions

2020 "Republic of Cynic", C-Lab, Taipei, Taiwan

2017 "Incarnation", Tina Keng Plus, Taipei, Taiwan

2014 "The Space That Remains: Yao Jui-Chung's Ruin Series", Church of Santa Maria della Pietà, Venice

2006 "Everything will Fall into Ruin", Taipei Fine Arts Museum, Taipei, Taiwan

1997 "Recover Mainland China-Prophecy & Action", Dimension Endowment of Art, Taipei, Taiwan

Selected Group Exhibitions

2018 "Shanghai Biennale", Switch Art Center, Shanghai, China

2016 "The 20th Biennale of Sydney", Carriageworks, Australia

2009 "Asia Pacific Triennial of Contemporary Art", Queensland Art Gallery, Brisbane, Australia

2005 "International Triennale of Contemporary Art YOKOHAMA 2005-Art Circus-Jumping from the Ordinary", Yokohama, Japan

1997 "La Biennale di Venezia", Palazzo delle Prigioni, Venice, Italy

洪譽豪 Yu-Hao Hung

學歷
國立臺灣藝術大學新媒體藝術研究所碩士

節選個展
2020「相位尋逕 - 洪譽豪個展」，大象藝術，臺中，臺灣
2018「流動的街區」，國立臺灣美術館，臺中，臺灣

節選聯展
2020「白晝之夜」，臺北，臺灣
2019「時間札記」，有章藝術博物館，臺北，臺灣
2019「高雄獎」，高雄市立美術館，高雄，臺灣
2018「虛擬花園─第六屆波蘭波茲南中介雙年展」，波茲南，波蘭
2018「全國美術展」，國立臺灣美術館，臺中，臺灣

Education
National Taiwan University of Arts, Master of New Media Arts

Selected Solo Exhibitions
2020 "Pathfinding between Phases-Yu-Hao Hung Solo
       Exhibition", Da Xiang Art Space, Taichung, Taiwan
2018 "On Fluid Street", National Taiwan Museum of Fine
       Arts, Taichung, Taiwan

Selected Group Exhibitions
2020 "Nuit Blanche Taipei", Taipei, Taiwan
2019 "A Note For Time", Yo-Chang Art Museum, New Taipei
       City, Taiwan
2019 "Kaohsiung Award", Kaohsiung Museum Of Fine Arts,
       Kaohsiung, Taiwan
2018 "Virtual Garden 6. Mediations Biennale", Poznan, Poland
2018 "National Art Exhibition, ROC", National Taiwan
       Museum of Fine Arts, Taichung, Taiwan

唐唐發 Tang Tang-Fa

學歷
2000 國立臺南藝術學院造形藝術研究所畢業
1991 文化大學美術系畢業

節選個展
2019「百貨裡的菜奇仔」，臺北敦南誠品 G 樓，臺北，臺灣
2017「擺攤 - 市場擺攤計畫」，臺北市士林區社子市場，臺北，臺灣
2015「公館擺攤ㄋㄟ」，苗栗公館鄉油桐花坊，苗栗，臺灣
2013「生活在藝術中，藝術中有生活」，海洋大學藝文中心
2007「過的不好」，關渡美術館，臺北，臺灣

節選聯展
2020「藝術走廊 Art Point」，臺南市美術館，臺南，臺灣
2019「asia in Asia – close by far away drums」，慶尚南道立美
       術館，南韓
2017「硬蕊／悍圖」，國立臺灣美術館，臺中，臺灣
2016「類似過於喧囂的孤獨─新樂園 20 年紀念展」，北師美術館，
       臺北，臺灣
2014「普普藝術＋工廠 - 熱塑、冷壓、當代台灣」，高雄市立美術館，
       高雄，臺灣

Education
2000 Graduate Institute of Plastic Arts, Tainan National
       University of the Arts
1991 Department of Fine Arts, Chinese Culture University

Selected Solo Exhibitions
2019 "A Marketplace in the Department Store", Eslite
       Dunnan Store Floor G, Taipei, Taiwan
2017 "Market Vendors Plans", Shezi Market, Taipei, Taiwan
2015 "Gongguan Vendor Hey!", Tung Lodge - Miaoli Branch,
       Miaoli, Taiwan
2013 "Living in Art, Art in Living"，National Taiwan Ocean
       University Art Center
2007 "Having Bad Days", Kuandu Museum of Fine Arts,
       Taipei, Taiwan

Selected Group Exhibitions
2020 "Art Point", Tainan Art Museum, Tainan, Taiwan
2019 "asia in Asia – close by far away drums", Gyeongnam
       Art Museum, South Korea
2017 "Hardcore Rally", National Taiwan Museum of Fine
       Arts, Taichung, Taiwan
2016 "Too Loud a Solitude", Museum of National Taipei
       University of Education, Taipei, Taiwan
2014 "Heating · Cooling: Contemporary Art in Taiwan",
       Kaohsiung Museum of Fine Arts, Kaohsiung, Taiwan

FIDATI (PINDY WINDY)

1985 出生於印尼
2004 高中畢業主修會計
2006 來臺灣擔任看護工作 9 年
2013 開始學習捏麵人，至今多次參加捏麵人展出和教學活動，
     並以印尼移工代表和個人身分獲得諸多獎項

1985 Born in Indonesia
2004 Graduated High School, Majored in Accounting
2006 Immigrated to Taiwan to work as a caretaker for 9 years
2013 Began learning tòhe. To this date has attended multiple
     tòhe exhibitions and educational activities, and has
     received multiple awards as a representative of
     Indonesian migrant workers.

張徐展 ZHANG XU zhan

學歷
2016 畢業於國立臺北藝術大學新媒體藝術研究所

節選個展
2017 「Si So Mi」，就在藝術空間，臺北，臺灣
2015 「自卑的蝙蝠─張徐展個展」，台北數位藝術中心，臺北，臺灣
2012 「陰極射線管的神祕儀式」，國立臺灣美術館，臺中，臺灣

節選聯展
2020 「第七屆日本橫濱三年展」，橫濱美術館，橫濱，日本
2019 「Jeune Création Internationale─第 15 屆法國里昂雙年
     展」，維勒班當代藝術中心，法國
2018 「上海雙年展─禹步」，上海當代藝術博物館，上海，中國
2015 「第五屆亞洲藝術雙年展」，國立臺灣美術館，臺中，臺灣
2012 「第七屆亞太當代藝術三年展」，昆士蘭現代美術館，昆士蘭，
     澳洲

Education
2016 Taipei National University of the Arts, New Media Art,
     Taipei, Taiwan (MFA)

Selected Solo Exhibitions
2017 "Si So Mi - ZHANG XU Zhan Solo Exhibition", Project
     Fulfill Art Space, Taipei, Taiwan
2015 "Inferiority Bat", Taipei digital art center, Taiwan
2012 "Ritual of Cathode Ray Tube", National Taiwan Museum
     of Fine Arts, Taichung, Taiwan

Selected Group Exhibitions
2020 "The 7th Yokohama Triennial", Yokohama, Japan
2019 "Jeune création internationale, 15e Biennale de Lyon",
     Institut d'art contemporain, Villeurbanne, Rhône-Alpes,
     France
2018 "The 12th Shanghai Biennale", Power Station of Art
     (PSA) , Shanghai, China
2015 "The 5th Asian Art Biennial", National Taiwan Museum
     of Fine Arts, Taichung, Taiwan
2012 "The 7th Asia Pacific Triennial of Contemporary Art
     -APT7 Cinema", Gallery of Modern Art and Queensland
     Art Gallery, Queensland, Australia

梁廷毓 Liang Ting-Yu

國立臺北藝術大學藝術跨領域研所碩士，主要以地理性調查、田野研究，論述書寫、結合計畫性的藝術行動、複合媒體實踐，關注鬼魂與地理、歷史、記憶與族群關係等議題，並以組織連結、展演、動態影像集、製圖、研討會、工作坊、文論等形式，進行跨領域問題場域與藝術界域的開展。

節選展覽
2019「墳・屍骨・紅壤層」個展，福利社，臺北，臺灣
2019「烏鬼」，台北當代藝術館，臺北，臺灣
2018「番肉考」個展，眾藝術，桃園，臺灣
2018「山、殺人、斷頭河」個展，水谷藝術，臺北，臺灣
2017「復甦術」聯展，中心新村，臺北，臺灣

Liang received his master's degree in trans-disciplinary arts from Taipei National University of Arts. Liang's practice focuses on integrating regional investigations and studies with project-based art actions and mixed media art. He examines issues related to historical archives and ethnic relations, and has recently expanded into exploring archives and local myths and legends. Using motion images, local ghost stories, image production, and writing, he creates art that looks into relationships between ghosts and topography.

Selected Exhibitions
2019 "Necropolis・Necro・The Red Soil" (solo exhibition), FreeS Art Space, Taipei, Taiwan
2019 "Stories We Tell To Scare Ourselves With", MOCA Taipei, Taipei, Taiwan
2018 "A History of Anthropophagy" (solo exhibition), Zone ART, Taoyuan, Taiwan
2018 "Mountain scene, Sha ran and Beheaded stream" (solo exhibition), Waley Art, Taipei, Taiwan
2017 "CPR joint exhibition", Heart Village, Taipei, Taiwan

許惠晴 HSU, HUI-CHING

目前就讀於國立臺灣師範大學美術系博士班新媒體科技藝術組

節選個展
2019「穿版仙女」，新樂園藝術空間，臺北，臺灣
2015「兒童新樂園」，新樂園藝術空間，臺北，臺灣
2014「我還在想」，In Live，臺北，臺灣
2012「對或錯」，新樂園藝術空間，臺北，臺灣
2010「意外墜落的延續」，新樂園藝術空間，臺北，臺灣

節選聯展
2019「複眼時代－ 第五屆機動眼國際動態媒體藝術節」，西昌 134 藝術空間，臺北，臺灣
2018「超機體－ 2018 第十三屆臺北數位藝術節」，松山文創園區，臺北，臺灣
2017「行・觀・遊・居」，國立臺灣美術館，臺中，臺灣
2008「永恆的成人遊戲工廠－新樂園十週年特展」，關渡美術館，臺北，臺灣
2002「歡樂迷宮」，高雄市立美術館，高雄，臺灣

Currently studying in the Ph. D. Program of New Media Arts and Technology, Department of Fine Arts, National Taiwan Normal University

Selected Solo Exhibitions
2019 "Angels Wear Blessings", SLY Art, Taipei, Taiwan
2015 "The Children's New Paradise", SLY Art, Taipei, Taiwan
2014 "I Am Thinking…", In Live, Taipei, Taiwan
2012 "Right or Wrong", SLY Art, Taipei, Taiwan
2010 "After the Accident", SLY Art, Taipei, Taiwan

Selected Group Exhibitions
2019 "The Era of Compound Eyes — RANDOMIZE Intl. Unstable Media Art Festival", Xichang 134 Art Space, Taipei, Taiwan
2018 "Trans Robotics — 13th Digital Art Festival Taipei 2018", Songshan Cultural and Creative Park, Taipei, Taiwan
2017 "To Roam, View, Travel and Live – An Immersive Experience of Ink Wash Painting", National Taiwan Museum of Fine Art, Taichung, Taiwan
2008 "ENTERNAL ADVENTURELAND", Kuandu Museum of Fine Arts, Taipei, Taiwan
2002 "Labyrinth of Pleasure", Kaohsiung Museum of Fine Arts, Kaohsiung, Taiwan

郭俞平 Kuo Yu-Ping

學歷

2008 畢業於臺灣藝術大學雕塑學系

2016 畢業於臺北藝術大學跨領域藝術研究所

節選個展

2019 「一盞燈進入房子，看不到其他房子」，台北當代藝術中心，
　　　臺北，臺灣

2019 「昨日有多真實」，TKG+ Projects，臺北，臺灣

2017 「小黑書」，谷公館，臺北，臺灣

2015 「中山高」，谷公館，臺北，臺灣

2013 「水泥之愛」，南海藝廊，臺北，臺灣

節選聯展

2018 「野根莖— 2019 臺灣雙年展」，國立臺灣美術館，臺中，臺灣

2018 「黑船、文明、芻言和 _____ 的足跡：從近代日本到東亞當代
　　　藝術」，日動畫廊，臺北，臺灣

2017 「菸葉、地毯、便當、紡織機、穴居人：當代藝術中的工藝及
　　　技術敘事」，鳳甲美術館，臺北，臺灣

2017 「熱帶氣旋」，關渡美術館，臺北，臺灣

2017 「伏流・書寫」，臺北市立美術館，臺北，臺灣

Education

2008 BA Sculpture, Taiwan University of the Arts

2016 MA, Institute of Interdisciplinary Art, Taipei University
　　　of the Arts

Selected Solo Exhibitions

2019 "There Is a Light That Enters Houses With No Other
　　　House In Sight", Taipei Contemporary Art Center,
　　　Taipei, Taiwan

2019 "How Real Is Yesterday", TKG+ Projects, Taipei, Taiwan

2017 "My Little Black Book", Michael Ku Gallery, Taipei, Taiwan

2015 "Sun Yat-San Freeway", Michael Ku Gallery, Taipei, Taiwan

2013 "Cement Love", Nan-hai Art Gallery, Taipei, Taiwan

Selected Group Exhibitions

2018 "Wild Rhizome-2018 Taiwan Biennial", National Taiwan
　　　Museum of Fine Arts, Taichung, Taiwan

2018 "Black Ships, Civilization, Remarks, and _____s'
　　　Footprints: From Japanese Modern to East Asian
　　　Contemporary Art", Galerie Niched Taipei, Taipei, Taiwan

2017 "Tobacco, Carpet, Lunch Box, Textile Machinery and
　　　Cave Men: the narratives of craftsmanship and
　　　technologies in contemporary art", Hong-Gah Museum,
　　　Taipei, Taiwan

2017 "Tropical Cyclone", Kuandu Museum, Taipei, Taiwan

2017 "RIVERRUN", Taipei Fine Arts Museum, Taipei, Taiwan

郭奕臣 KUO I-Chen

學歷

畢業於國立臺北藝術大學科技藝術研究所

節選個展

2019 「實踐街 1 號登月計畫」，臺灣當代文化實驗場，臺北，臺灣

2017 「STUPIN.ORG」耿畫廊，臺北，臺灣

2015 「伊通公園」，伊通公園，臺北，臺灣

2013 「Home-Less is More」，456 藝廊，紐約，美國

2011 「光年」，臺北市立美術館，臺北，臺灣

節選聯展

2020 「白晝之夜」，臺北，臺灣

2018 「未來簡史 2050」，國立臺灣美術館，臺中，臺灣

2016 「朗誦／文件：台北雙年展 1996-2014」，臺北市立美術館，
　　　臺北，臺灣

2008 「第 16 屆雪梨雙年展：革命 - 轉動的形式」，雪梨，澳洲

2005 「第五十一屆威尼斯雙年展臺灣館：自由的幻象」，臺灣館，
　　　普里奇歐尼宮，威尼斯，義大利

Education

MFA in New Media Art, Taipei National University of the Arts

Selected Solo Exhibitions

2019 "Shijian st. 1 Landing Program", Taiwan Contemporary
　　　Culture Lab, Taipei, Taiwan

2017 "STUPIN.ORG", TKG+ Projects, Taipei, Taiwan

2015 "IT Park", IT Park, Taipei, Taiwan

2013 "Home-Less is More", 456 Gallery, New York, USA

2011 "Lightyears", Taipei Fine Arts Museum, Taipei, Taiwan

Selected Group Exhibitions

2020 "Nuit Blanche Taipei", Taipei, Taiwan

2018 "2050, A Brief History of the Future", National Taiwan
　　　Museum of Fine Arts, Taichung, Taiwan

2016 "Declaration / Documentation: Taipei Biennial, 1996-
　　　2014", Taipei Fine Arts Museum, Taipei, Taiwan

2008 "The 16th Biennale of Sydney: REVOLUTIONS-
　　　FORMSTHAT TURN", Sydney, Australia

2005 "51th Venice Biennial", Taiwan pavilion , Prigioni,
　　　Venice, Italy

陳伯義 Chen Po-I

節選個展

2019 「第 4 屆臺南傑出藝術家巡迴展－交陪大舞台：陳伯義 × 吳其
錚雙個展」，臺南文化中心、高雄文化中心、臺北中正紀念堂、
宜蘭文化中心、臺中大墩文化中心、新營文化中心，臺灣

2019 「食炮人」，非常廟藝文空間，臺北，臺灣

2016 「後莫拉克」，非畫廊，臺北，臺灣

2013 「紅毛港遷村實錄一家」，關渡美術館，臺北，臺灣

節選聯展

2019 「新神劇場」，Rossi & Rossi Gallery，香港，中國

2018 「告訴我一個故事：地方性與敘事」，山德雷托‧雷‧雷包登戈
基金會，杜林，義大利

2017 「近未來的交陪：2017 蕭壠國際當代藝術節」，蕭壠藝文中心，
臺南，臺灣

2016 「傾圮的明日」，歐洲攝影之家，巴黎，法國

Selected Solo Exhibitions

2019 "The Great Stage of Kau-Puê — A Due Exhibition
by Chen Po-I×Wu Chi-Zeng", Tainan Cultural Center;
Kaohsiung Cultural Center ; Chiang Kai-Shek Memorial
Hall ; Yilan Cultural Center ; Taichung City Dadun
Cultural Center ; Xinying Cultural Center, Taiwan

2019 "Firework Baptist", VT Artsalon, Taipei, Taiwan

2016 "Post-Morakot", Beyond Gallery, Taipei, Taiwan

2013 "Records of the Relocation of Hongmaogang Village",
Kuandu Museum of Fine Arts, Taipei, Taiwan

Selected Group Exhibitions

2019 "Theatre of New Gods", Rossi & Rossi Gallery, Hong
Kong, China

2018 "Love in the Fallen City", Hsinchu City Art Gallery,
Hsinchu, Taiwan

2017 "Kau-Puê, Mutual Companionship in Near Future: 2017
Soulangh International Contemporary Art Festival",
Soulangh Cultural Park, Tainan, Taiwan

2016 "Lendemain Chagrin", Maison Européenne de la
Photographie, Paris, France

陳宣誠 Eric Chen

1978 年出生於臺南，現居住及工作於臺南、臺中、桃園。國立臺南
藝術大學藝術博士，現為中原大學建築系專任助理教授、馬來西亞
UCSI 建築系客座教授、共感地景創作｜ArchiBlur Lab 主持建築
師。長期探索在身體與地景間發展另一種重新定義建築的尺度，企圖
用最真實的身體感，反覆的去體會事物最根本的價值，讓建築成為一
種關於人與非人的環境。主要的創作實踐為：2014 臺北市立美術館
「X-Site 計畫」的《邊緣地景》、2015 瀨戶內藝術祭家屋計畫《屋橋》、
《城市浮洲計畫》、馬來西亞《綠洲聚落計畫》，法國《懸山‧浮橋》，
馬來西亞《懸山》以及 2016 台北雙年展、2017 夏伽雙年展《共感
群體》、巴勒斯坦美術館《存在的邊界》、2019《麻豆糖業大地藝術祭》
總策展 … 等。

Born in Tainan in 1978 and currently residing and working
in Tainan, Taichung, and Taoyuan, Eric Chen holds the PhD
degree of Arts from Tainan National University of the Arts,
and now he is the full-time assistant professor of Department
of Architecture, Chung Yuan Christian University, visiting
professor of Department of Architecture, UCSI in Malaysia,
and chief architect of ArchiBlur Lab. His creative practices
over the past years are the use of body anatomy as reference
for expressing group senses, building generation, urban
landscape, island manufacturing, thinking, and ideas in an
attempt to develop a method to explore the issues in an open
framework. He has engaged in the long-term exploration on
body and landscapes in order to develop another redefined
architectural scale. He also attempts to repeatedly perceive
the most fundamental value of everything with the most
authentic body feelings, which enables buildings to become
a kind of human environment. His main creative practices
are: "Landscape of the Boundary" of 2014 "X-Site Project"
, "Bridge House" of 2015 Setouchi Triennale "Art House
Project" , "Urban Archipelago Project," "Oasis Settlement
Project" in Malaysia, "Floating Mountains‧Suspended
bridge" in France, "Floating Mountains" in Malaysia, 2016
Taipei Biennale, 2017 Sharjah Biennial "Collectivism",
"Threshold of Being" at Palestine Art Museum, Chief curator
of 2019 "Madou Sugar Industry Art Triennial", etc.

陳毅哲 Yi-Che, Chen

學歷
2018 畢業於國立臺北藝術大學美創所複媒組
2014 畢業於國立臺北藝術大學美術系版畫組

個展
2019 「類工廠：陳崑山 & 陳毅哲」，綠鏡藝廊，臺灣
2017 「十八巷五號，我回來了！」，永富五號，淡水，臺灣
2016 「Now , please turn on the light , We are going to close.」，十八巷五號，淡水，臺灣
2015 「測量兩個地方」，十八巷五號，淡水，臺灣
2014 「假皮：脫離剩餘的島」，美術系館 F302，臺北，臺灣

聯展
2018 「痕跡超渡所」，Instant 42，彰化，臺灣
2014 「半年勞動計畫：駐居」，十八巷五號，淡水，臺灣
2014 「別讓我傷心！」，地下美術館，臺北，臺灣
2013 「FACTORY 陳毅哲 & 陳書平」，8 又 2/1 畫廊，臺北，臺灣
2013 「早春圖」二零一三藝術新星，世界畫廊，臺中，臺灣

Education
2018 M.F.A in Fine Arts, Taipei National University of the Arts
2014 B.F.A. Department of Fine Arts, Taipei National University of the Arts

Selected Solo Exhibitions
2019 "Quasi - Factory : Father to Son", Rhythm Art Gallery, Taiwan
2017 "No.5, Lane18, I'm Back!", YunFu Studio, Tamsui, Taiwan
2016 "Now, please turn on the light, We are going to close.", No.5, Lane18, Taiwan
2015 "Measuring Two Place", No.5, Lane18, Taiwan
2014 "False Skin: Separate the last Islands", Fine Arts F302, Taiwan

Selected Group Exhibitions
2018 "Transcending the Passage of Time", Instant 42, Taiwan
2015 "A Half Year Labor : Residence", No.5, Lane18, Taiwan
2014 "Don't make me sad! ", Underground Experimental Museum, Taipei, Taiwan
2013 "Factory Yi-Che,Chen & Shu-Ping, Chen", 8½ Gallery, Taichung, Taiwan
2013 "Early Spring Pictures", 2013 Art Stars, World Gallery, Taipei, Taiwan

黃彥超 Huang Yen-Chao

1985 年生於臺灣，2011 年獲取高雄獎 - 首獎，並與友人共同成立了創作工作室 - 掀牆，且頻繁發表展演與沙龍。

作品思考當代身體的可能性，想像自己的身體彷彿被通電了，因而有了「感應器」、「接收器」、「處理器」的想像，並且開啟了許多關於 - 身體、與表演之間的來回，與探詢。
將自己的身體想像為一原點中心，許多能量從四面八方朝奔我而來。

2011 高雄獎 首獎
2012 臺北美術獎 優選
2014 臺南新藝獎 首獎
2018 與野孩子肢體劇場合作 繁花聖母 (獲臺新藝術獎提名)
2020 空總 c_ lab 直播創作 快感指令 - 第三現場

Born in 1985, Huang Yen-Chao was nominated by many significant art prizes in Taiwan, including Kaohsiung Art Prize. Since 2018 he runs an artist collective studio/ independent art space, which is called "Open Wide."

He perceives body as basic unit and creates multidiscipline art form and considering a mixed body experience due to the impact of contemporary diverse artistic medium. Many form are been created due to this concept. The early stage of his creation: Electronic Communication Man that indicates the contemporary living has been electrified. Our life seems to become a visual scape with a layer of wave. Most works have been created is painting on the room wall from that stage.

Then he transformed body consciousness, and use plastic and waste material as its foundation to think many possible extensions of body. With theatre group, "L'Enfant S. Physical Theatre", he was working with them closely and recreated together Genet's play, Our Lady of the Flowers, for the stage to discuss how we can think on morality, lust, gender, while Taiwan is becoming a more gender equality country. (This theater performance is nominated by Taishin Arts Awards.)

Recently he conceived his latest work from his painting background, that if we see our daily route in google map, especially Uber eat drivers' route, then it could be perceived as painting activity in everyday life.

鄧堯鴻 Deng Yau-Horng

學歷
1991 畢業於中國文化大學美術系

節選個展
2019 「繭影，一個又白又大的痰——」，邊境黑白切，新竹，臺灣
2016 「水在水中，水守護著秘密」，89 工作室，關西，臺灣
2013 「剩餘與蔥翠」，Z 書房，臺中，臺灣
2011 「月明星稀」，光之藝廊，臺中，臺灣
2010 「於一剎那間照見過往一切」，苳樂藝術空間，臺中，臺灣

節選聯展
2019 「記憶河流」，宜蘭人故事館，宜蘭，臺灣
2019 「魂過成灰」，七沁空間，關西，臺灣
2018 「再基地，當實驗成為態度——」，臺灣當代文化實驗場，
     臺北，臺灣
2017 「羞恥的修辭」，關渡美術館，臺北，臺灣
2015 「Wall to Wall 素描排練」，Z 書房，臺中，臺灣

Education
1991 B.A., Department of Fine Arts, Chinese Culture
     University, Taipei, Taiwan

Selected Solo Exhibitions
2019 "Shadow of a Cocoon, A white and big sputum",
     Frontier Space, Hsinchu, Taiwan
2016 "Water in water, Water keeps the secret", 89 studio,
     Guanxi, Taiwan
2013 "The Surplus and the Lushness", Z Space, Taichung,
     Taiwan
2011 "Bright Moon Accompanied by Sparse Stars",
     Luminance Art Space, Taichung, Taiwan
2010 "Seeing the past in sudden moment", Espace Liu,
     Taichung, Taiwan

Selected Group Exhibitions
2019 "The River Memories", Yilan Story Museum, Yilan,
     Taiwan
2019 "Soul Ash", Qi Qin Space, Guanxi, Taiwan
2018 "Re-Base: When Experiments Become Attitude —— ",
     Taiwan Contemporary Culture Lab, Taipei, Taiwan
2017 "Rhetoric of Shame", Kuandu Museum fo Fine Arts,
     Taipei, Taiwan
2015 "Wall to Wall", Z Space, Taichung, Taiwan

鄧雯馨 Teng Wen Hsin

學歷
2015 畢業於國立臺灣藝術大學多媒體動畫藝術學系新媒體藝術
     碩士班

節選個展
2018 「超時空 WiFi」，RAW Art Space，吉隆坡，馬來西亞
2016 「Blue Tears」，國立臺灣美術館，臺中，臺灣
2015 「水中夢遊」，水谷藝術，臺北，臺灣
2013 「悖光。Rebel Light 李亞唐 x 鄧雯馨雙個展」，板橋四三五藝
     文特區，臺北，臺灣

節選聯展
2019 「複眼時代—第五屆機動眼國際動態媒體藝術節」，西昌 134 空
     間，臺北，臺灣
2018 「第 14 屆雅典數位藝術節—世界藝術節」，雅典音樂廳，雅典，
     希臘
2016 「第 7 屆西班牙馬德里現代數位科影音藝術節」，希貝雷絲宮，
     馬德里，西班牙
2015 「亞洲實驗電影與行為藝術系列：臺灣」，韓國國立現代美術館
     高陽駐留專案空間，首爾，南韓
2014 「第 27 屆法國馬賽錄像藝術節」，La Friche Belle de Mai，
     馬賽，法國

Education
2015 Graduate Institute of New Media Arts, National Taiwan
     University of Arts

Selected Solo Exhibitions
2018 "Transcendental Conversation", RAW Art Space, Kuala
     Lumpur, Malaysia
2016 "Blue Tears", National Taiwan Museum of Fine Arts,
     Taichung, Taiwan
2015 "Sleep in the water", Waley Art, Taipei, Taiwan
2013 "Rebel Light", Banqiao 435 Art Zone, Taipei, Taiwan

Selected Group Exhibitions
2019 "The Era of Compound Eyes—RANDOMIZE Intl.
     Unstable Media Art Festival", Xichang 134, Taipei, Taiwan
2018 "The 14th Athens Digital Arts Festival- Festivels of the
     world", Megaron - The Athens Concert Hall, Athens,
     Greece
2016 "MADATAC 07", CentroCentroCibeles, Madrid, Spain
2015 "Asian Experimental Film & Performance Art",
     National Museum of Modern and Contemporary Art/
     Goyang, Seoul, Korea
2014 "27th Festival Les Instants Vidéo", Friche la Belle de
     Mai, Marseille, France

顏忠賢　Yan Chung-Hsien

藝術家。小說家。策展人。實踐大學建築設計系前系主任、現專任教授。美國紐約 MOMA/PS1 駐館藝術家，臺北駐耶路撒冷、加拿大交換藝術家，藝術、設計作品曾赴多國參加展覽，曾為臺灣設計博覽會、台北市公共藝術節、台北當代藝術館「小碎花不」諸展覽之策展人。出版小說、詩、散文、影評、書評、設計評論、藝術作品集、建築評論三十餘本書：《三寶西洋鑑》、《寶島大旅社》、《殘念》、《老天使俱樂部》、《壞設計達人》、《時髦讀書機器》、《偷偷混亂：一個不前衛藝術家在紐約的一年》、《明信片旅行主義》《巴黎與台北的密談》、《J-WALK 我的耶路撒冷症候群》、《J-SHOT 我的耶路撒冷陰影》《世界盡頭》、《雲，及其不明飛行物》、《鬼畫符》、《刺身》、《壞迷宮》、《阿賢》、《軟建築》等書。

Artist, writer, curator, designer, professor, Ex-chairman, Architecture Department of Shih-Chien University. Taipei Award Winner of MoMA PS1, New York, International Artist Studio Program, Selected as the visiting Artist to Canada, Jerusalem/Taipei Artist Residence Program, Representative of Taipei in Asian Arts Network. Published thirty Books: 〈Soft Architecture〉, 〈Bad Maze〉....e.t.c.

穿孔城市 = Perforated city／駱麗真總編輯・—— 初版・——
臺北市：財團法人臺北市文化基金會台北當代藝術館，2020.12
192 面；18 x 25 公分
中英對照
ISBN 978-986-98966-5-8（平裝）
1. 當代藝術 2. 作品集

902   109021717

專輯執行

發行者：財團法人台北市文化基金會
總編輯：駱麗真
執行編輯：王雪妮、劉逸萱
美術編輯：魏妏如、陳彥如
攝影：王世邦
翻譯：黃亮融、游騰緯、張韜

出版者：財團法人台北市文化基金會台北當代藝術館
地址：103 臺北市大同區長安西路 39 號
電話：+886-2-2552-3721
傳真：+886-2-2559-3874
網址：www.mocataipei.org.tw
印刷：奇異多媒體印藝有限公司
定價：新台幣 800 元
初版一刷：2020 年 12 月
ISBN：978-986-98966-5-8
本專刊編輯著作權屬於臺北市政府文化局所有

台北當代藝術館團隊

館長：駱麗真
副館長：張玉漢

展覽組
組長：王雪妮
副組長：許翼翔、黃俊璋
專員：阮楨鈞、劉逸萱、廖珮�

視覺設計組
組長：蘇丰健
專員：楊子慧、鍾易廷

教育推廣與發展行銷組
組長：高慈敏、呂易穎
副組長：許格元
專員：陳筱筠、林育華、謝瑜薰、林俐瑄、張耀月

行政組
組長：曾清琪
副組長：李金玉
專員：郭宜茵、周倪萱、陳貞蓉、陳忠成

研究組
專員：黃香凝、張數滿、詹話宇、林懷亞

Editorial Team

Publisher: Taipei Culture Foundation
Chief Editor: LiChen Loh
Executive Editors: Shirney Wong, Yi-Hsuan Liu
Designers: Wenru Wei, Yanru Chen
Photographer: Anpis Wang
Translators: Liang-jung Huang, Tony Yu, Ey Chang

Published by Taipei Culture Foundation / Museum of Contemporary Art, Taipei
Address: No. 39, Chang-An West Road, Taipei, Taiwan
Telephone: +886-2-2552-3721
Fax: +886-2-2559-3874
Website: www.mocataipei.org.tw
Printed by CHIYI MEDIA PRINTING CO., LTD.
Price: TWD800
First Published in December, 2020
ISBN: 978-986-98966-5-8
Copyright by the Department of Cultural Affairs, Taipei City Government, all rights reserved.

MOCA Team

Director: LiChen Loh
Deputy Director: Yu-Han Chang

Department of Exhibition
Supervisor: Shirney Wong
Deputy Supervisors: Ian Yi-Hsiang Hsu, Gino Huang
Specialists: Mia Ruan, Yi-Hsuan Liu, Pei-Yu Liao

Department of Visual Design
Supervisor: Feng-Jian Su
Specialists: Lacy Yang, Yi-Ting Chung

Department of Education and Communications
Supervisors: Beatrice Kao, Yi-ying Lu
Deputy Supervisor: Ke-yuan Hsu
Specialists: Xiao-yun Chen, Yuhua Lin, Yuhsun Hsieh, Lihsuan Lin, Yao-Yueh Chang

Department of Administration
Supervisor: Kate Tseng
Deputy Supervisor: Erika Li
Specialists: Vivian Kuo, Annie Chou, Anita Chen, Ryan Chen

Department of Research
Specialists: Anita Hsiang-Ning Huang, Shuman Chang, Huatzu Chan, Huai-ya Lin

指導單位
Supervisor

台北市文化局

主辦單位
Organizers

贊助單位
Supporting Sponsors

特別感謝
Special Thanks

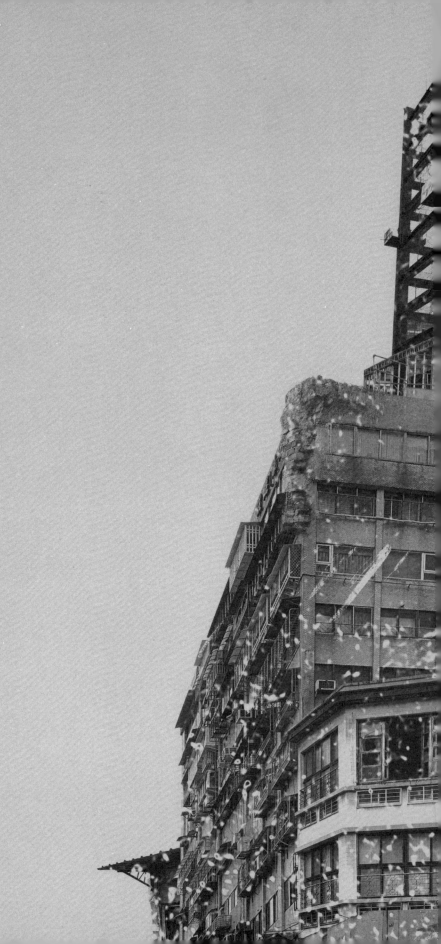